THE ODD SISTERS

A TALE OF THE THREE WITCHES

THE
ODD SISTERS
A TALE OF THE THREE WITCHES

BY SERENA VALENTINO

DISNEP PRESS

LOS ANGELES • NEW YORK

INTERIOR ILLUSTRATIONS BY

Pablo Santander Tiozzo-Lyon

Printed in the United States of America
First Hardcover Edition, July 2019
10 9 8 7 6 5 4 3 2 1
ISBN 978-1-368-01318-5
FAC-020093-19137
Library of Congress Control Number: 2019934306
This book is set in 13-point Garamond 3 LT Pro.
www.disneybooks.com

Dedicated to Tom Waits

I will search every face for Lucinda's
And she will go off with me down to hell
      —Tom Waits, "Lucinda"

Forbidden Mountain
(Maleficent's Fortress)

Morningstar
Kingdom

The
Cyclopean
Mountains

The
Lighthouse
of the
Gods

Ursula's Underwater
Realm

Snow White's
Castle

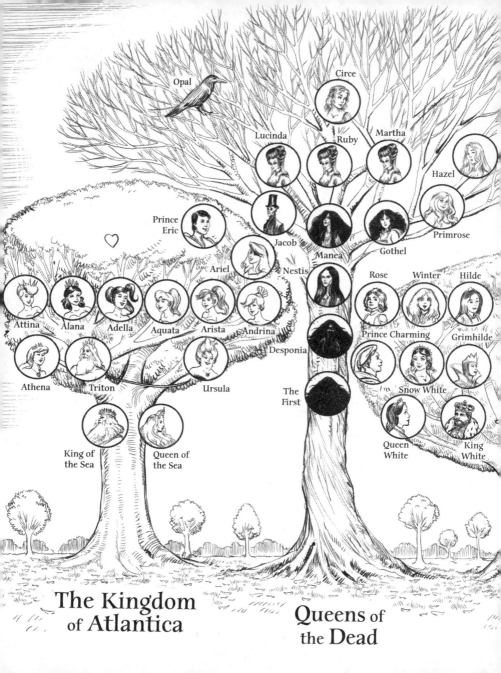

Opal

Circe

Lucinda   Ruby   Martha

Hazel

Jacob   Manea   Gothel   Primrose

Prince
Eric

Ariel   Nestis

Rose   Winter   Hilde

Attina   Alana   Adella   Aquata   Arista   Andrina

Prince Charming   Grimhilde

Athena   Triton   Ursula   Desponia

Snow White

The
First

King of
the Sea   Queen of
the Sea

Queen
White   King
White

The Kingdom
of Atlantica

Queens of
the Dead

Belle ♥ Beast

Aurora

Tulip

Maleficent

King
Stephan

Queen
Leah

Queen
Morningstar

King
Morningstar

Nanny

Fairy
Godmother

Merryweather

Fauna

Flora

Blue Fairy

Circe

Lucinda

Ruby

Martha

Oberon

Lady Lily

The White
Family

The Fairylands

THE ODD SISTERS

A TALE OF THE THREE WITCHES

PROLOGUE

My mothers, Lucinda, Ruby, and Martha, are by definition odd, and they are sisters. Identical triplet sisters, to be exact.

Many have remarked on their appearance over the years. The Dark Fairy, Maleficent, thought they were the most bewitching creatures she had ever seen. Others have compared them to broken, neglected dolls left out in the wind and rain to crack and fade. The most thoughtful observation was made by the great and terrible sea witch Ursula. She said the odd sisters' beauty was so entirely out of proportion it made them compellingly grotesque.

1

I always found them beautiful, even in their mania. Even when they made me angry. Even now, disappointed and heartbroken by them, knowing just how cruel, destructive, and foul they really are. I still love them.

In reading my mothers' journals, Snow White and I have learned there is no witch alive who is more powerful than my mothers—except for one. Me.

If you are acquainted with the odd sisters' story, then you know long ago they had a little sister named Circe who was tragically killed when the Dark Fairy, Maleficent, destroyed the Fairylands in a fit of rage on her sixteenth birthday. This was a secret they kept from Maleficent. Lucinda, Ruby, and Martha were so desperate to bring their little sister back to life that they gave up the very best parts of themselves to create a new Circe. A replacement for the sister they had lost.

Me.

I was no longer their sister, but their daughter, a daughter created by magic and by love. My mothers would do anything to protect me—and they have, unflinchingly, over the ages. They've wreaked havoc and chaos, destroying everyone and everything in their path all in the name of protecting me. Their Circe.

All my life I believed them to be my sisters, and they were there to watch over me, keeping me safe, even from the smallest things. I always thought they were just doting and protective older siblings because they were forced to raise me as their own daughter after something horrible happened to our parents, something too awful to tell me about. While we were growing up, Lucinda, Ruby, and Martha refused to tell me about our mother and father. They said they were protecting me from the truth. But the truth was they were my mothers.

Growing up with such protective mothers was a challenge. But their unwavering love and willingness to share their spell craft made me thrive magically. From a young age I could do magic that older witches could not, and my mothers always remarked that they thought my gifts were stronger than even their own. As I got older I realized they might be right, because I was constantly surprised by my ability to do spells and cast magic so effortlessly. The problem is that it never occurs to me. More times than not, someone will have to bring it to my attention, the idea of using magic, or the fact that I've just performed a spell or magical feat without even knowing it. My mothers were always there to remind me and to protect me from any harm that might come to me.

It wasn't until I was a bit older and found myself in love with the Beast Prince that my mothers' overprotectiveness became brutal and vindictive. The Prince broke my heart, and my mothers, well, they wanted to destroy him in return.

I remember the day I told them I had fallen in love, and how they flew into a panic. They convinced me to partake in a ruse that would prove to me this man wasn't worthy of me. I went along because I trusted his devotion to me and I would do anything to convince them of his honest intentions. So I dressed like a pig farmer's daughter, and I mucked around with the beasts and waited for my prince to find me. It was he who ended up being a beast. He reacted exactly as the odd sisters had expected. He was disgusted by me and withdrew his love. He was so vile and so cruel to me I cursed him.

With every foul deed he committed, it would be written on his face. If he changed his ways, then the curse would not mar his appearance. I gave him an enchanted rose from his garden to remind him of the love we once had together. When the last petal dropped, he would remain in the form of his own design forever.

Like many witches and fairies before me, I gave him a chance to break the curse by finding and receiving true love. I thought it was fair. I thought I was giving him the opportunity to redeem himself. But the odd sisters had other designs. They drove him mad and lured him to the path of destruction at every turn, making sure he would turn into the horrible beast they saw residing within him. All this I could have forgiven if they hadn't involved Princess Tulip Morningstar and Belle. My mothers drove the Beast insane with their constant torments.

He treated Princess Tulip so abominably and cruelly that she flung herself off the rocky cliffs and into the sea witch's tentacles. Ursula spared her life in exchange for her beauty and her voice. Well, I retrieved both for the poor princess, by trading them for Ursula's seashell necklace my mothers had magicked away from King Triton. I couldn't forgive them for putting Tulip's life in danger. And I couldn't forgive the horrors they put poor Belle through all in the name of destroying the Beast for his mistreatment of me.

This was just the beginning of my disappointments in my mothers, and the start of my new role: righting the wrongs they had committed. I was so angry with them for putting Tulip's and Belle's lives in danger that I went away, refusing their summons. I hid myself from them in every way I knew. It was the only means I had to punish them: withholding my love in hopes they would change their ways.

Frantic, my mothers called on Ursula for help. She was a powerful witch, and they thought she could help them find me. Little did they know she had kidnapped me and reduced me to a mere shell of myself, thrusting me into her dark garden with the other souls she had reaped over the ages. Ursula agreed to help my mothers if they promised to forge a spell in hate to bring down her brother, King Triton. Ursula was within her rights to take her brother's throne. Their father had left it to both of them, and Triton's treatment of Ursula was horrific. Had Ursula brought this plan to me, I would likely have rallied to her cause. But I would never have allowed myself to be bound in hate, or agreed to hurt Triton's youngest daughter, Ariel.

Maleficent, my mothers' longtime friend, warned them not to become entangled in Ursula's affairs. She warned them that Ursula couldn't be trusted, that the spell was dangerous. They didn't listen—as they often don't—ignoring the signs that Ursula wasn't the witch they had grown to love over the many years of their friendship. Blinded by their obsession with finding me, they went along with her mad plan to destroy Triton. All this I could have forgiven if they hadn't tried to kill Ariel.

Once my mothers found out Ursula had taken my soul and put me in her garden, they became enraged. They reversed the spell they had created in hate to rebound on Ursula, killing her and nearly destroying the lands and themselves in an attempt to save me. But they didn't anticipate what it would do to them. They couldn't predict that it would leave their bodies slumbering under the glass dome of the solarium in Morningstar and their souls residing in the dreamscape. That is where they remain to this day.

The magnitude of this spell brought Maleficent to Morningstar. She hoped to find someone powerful enough to make sure Prince Phillip would not break the sleeping curse she had placed on her daughter, Aurora, on the day of her christening. The curse was to take effect on her sixteenth birthday, which was fast approaching. Maleficent was afraid when Aurora turned sixteen, she would come into her powers, just as Maleficent had, in a blaze of anger and fire. She was terrified for her daughter and wanted to spare her the heartbreak of destroying everyone and everything she had ever loved, just as Maleficent had done.

I hadn't known that my mothers were so close to Maleficent, that they had known and loved her when she was young. I didn't know they helped her create a child: Aurora, Maleficent's shining star. A spell that would be Maleficent's ruin, as it has been my mothers' ruin since they created me in the same fashion. So I decided to keep my mothers in the dreamscape until I could determine what to do. All I asked of them was that they sit and be quiet and not meddle. I needed time to help in the aftermath of Ursula's and Maleficent's deaths and the destruction they had both caused with my mothers' assistance.

But they were not content with waiting. They were not content with sitting quietly while I cleaned up their messes. They meddled again, this time with Gothel, a childhood friend who was in need of their help. Gothel was a witch who lived in the dead woods with her sisters, Primrose and Hazel, and their powerful mother, Manea. While reading Gothel's story in the book of fairy tales, with every flip of a page, I learned more about my mothers' natures. I saw them as young witches full of potential and the capacity for loyal friendship—until they lost their little sister, Circe, the girl I used to be. That was when they started to change. The singular focus was on bringing her back to life. They succeeded, but the magic they used changed them. It changed me, too.

It led to their madness.

After that, every ounce of their beings was focused on protecting me. They refused to lose me again.

They used and strung along Gothel, making her feel as if they thought of her as a sister. They took her mother's spells from the dead woods and used them for their own aims. When Gothel's sisters were killed in an attack by their own mother, my mothers promised to help Gothel bring them back from the dead. My mothers swooped in, making promises I'm sure they never intended to keep, all the while plotting to take Gothel's magic rapunzel flower for themselves. Their goal was to restore Maleficent from the degenerative effects of the spell they had cast to create Aurora. Meanwhile, I am sure they blame Gothel for my anger, because I caught them meddling once again.

But the truth is it's not Gothel's fault. Nor is it Maleficent's, Ursula's, the Beast's, or Grimhilde's. The truth is I have had enough of the destruction and heartbreak caused by my mothers.

As I've witnessed this tangled web of events, following along with each story in the book of fairy tales, I've noticed a pattern. My mothers wish to do what they think is good and just—but only when it comes to protecting me. Those who get in their way meet with disaster. I want to forgive them, because I know in their hearts they believe what they are doing is right—and who wouldn't do anything to protect their child? But what I can't forgive is their utter lack of empathy or compassion for those they tried to destroy for simply standing in their way: Tulip. Belle. Maurice. And Snow White.

How they hate Snow White. The terrible things

they did to her as a child. Frightening her in the woods and tormenting her with threats of witchcraft. Then giving Grimhilde a mirror possessed by her abusive father, driving her insane, and encouraging her to kill her own daughter. It's unforgivable. And though they've trapped Grimhilde in the mirror her father used to haunt, they are still not satisfied. They still hate Snow White.

To this day, the reason remains a mystery to me.

So as I sit here writing in my mothers' journals, adding to their book of shadows, I wonder how I got here, and how I came to find such a friend in my cousin Snow White. Without her I don't know how I would have survived any one of these revelations. Without her I wouldn't have had the courage to see my mothers for who they are.

Snow has been my mirror and my guide as I watch her distance herself from her own destructive mother. A mother full of grief and despair over the treatment of her daughter. A mother forever pleading with her daughter for her forgiveness. Snow is burdened with the task of making her mother feel better for her past misdeeds, as I am burdened by my own mothers' treachery.

Finding each other has been such a gift to both of us. I feel stronger having Snow at my side as we search together for the truth about my past and my mothers' past.

Therefore, this is my story as much as it is Lucinda's, Ruby's, and Martha's. Because we are all one. Our fates are connected by a delicate silver thread, weaving us together, binding us by blood, by magic, and by a dangerous, all-encompassing love.

I sit here in my mothers' house and I wonder what to do next. Do I leave my mothers in the dreamscape to punish them for their crimes? Or do I unleash them on the many kingdoms only for them to ruin more lives, all in the name of love?

Even as I ask myself this, I already know the answer. It's become heartbreakingly clear I am responsible for my mothers' foul deeds. And there is only one thing to be done about it.

I just need to find the courage to bring myself to the task.

CHAPTER I

THE WITCH BEHIND THE MIRRORS

The odd sisters were caught in perpetual twilight.

In the land of dreams all was chaos, rhythm, and magic. Their mirrored chamber seemed smaller and more confined now that Circe had turned all their mirrors black. It was their punishment for the role they had played in Gothel's story, and for the deaths of Maleficent, Ursula, and the queen Grimhilde.

The odd sisters feared this time their daughter wouldn't forgive them as she had so many times in the past. They had crossed the line too many times. They had lost track of the many reasons Circe was banishing them to darkness and withholding her love. And it broke their hearts, sending them into fits of panic and rage. It reminded Lucinda of the promise she had made.

To destroy everyone Circe held dear.

The land of dreams had lost its magic for the sisters. They no longer heard the rhythm in the chaos. They could no longer break the code and use the magic there. The magic was in the many mirrors, but the mirrors were now dark to them. Circe had seen to that. The odd sisters were helpless, captive, and alone with their madness, taking them down a familiar path of ruin and despair.

Martha and Ruby sat on the floor of the chamber, crying. They still wore their tattered blood-stained dresses, clothes they had been wearing since they had done the blood ceremony to communicate with Maleficent when she was fighting Prince Phillip. It all seemed so long ago, but it had only just happened. They'd hardly had time to grieve their beloved dragon fairy-witch before they were distracted by Gothel's antics.

"Curse Gothel!" Lucinda screamed as she manically paced the circumference of the room. "If it hadn't been for her, Circe may have forgiven us!" Martha and Ruby were still crying, not listening to Lucinda's ravings. "And what if she learns the truth? What will she think of us then?" Lucinda looked down at her sisters. The three of them had always felt like one. Always the same. But for the briefest of moments, they seemed foreign to her. Almost freakish and unnatural, so different and apart from her. The feeling took her by surprise. She understood in that moment how Circe must see them now.

"Silence! Stop your weeping!" Lucinda needed quiet. She needed to think. She needed to find a way out of the chamber so she could get vengeance on the Fairy Godmother and her meddlesome sister, Nanny, for taking their Circe away from her. "I can't think with your endless wailing! I promise you, Sisters, we will find a way to destroy everything Circe holds dear! We need to find a means to lure Maleficent back to life so she can help us in our cause! She hates the fairies as much as we do!"

17

"Lucinda, no! This is exactly why Circe is angry with us!" screeched Ruby. She was looking up at Lucinda with her wide eyes. Lucinda could see the madness in them, and it frightened her.

"Yes, Lucinda!" Martha cried. "She will never forgive us if we kill them!"

"Shut up!" Lucinda abruptly stopped pacing and looked down at both of her deranged sisters. "If we take everything and everyone she loves, she will have no choice but to turn to us for comfort! We will be all she has left in the world. She will need us!" She felt as if she were pleading with senseless children.

"That didn't work with Gothel! What makes you think it will work with Circe?"

Lucinda considered Ruby's question. The fact was she wasn't sure it would work. But she felt they had no other choice before them.

"We neglected Gothel. We left her alone and she went mad. We didn't realize how much of Manea was within her." Lucinda looked as if she was remembering something, seeing it in her mind. She twitched her head as if trying to banish the thought. "Gothel was weak. Sisters in magic or no, she is nothing to us now! She refused to give us the flower so we could save Maleficent! She's to blame for Maleficent's death! Surely Circe will understand if we bring Maleficent back!"

"We should just wait," said Martha. "If we wait and do nothing, as Circe asked, she will forgive us eventually. She has to!"

Lucinda waved her hand at her sisters, forgetting they no longer had magic in this place. "Silence! I will not wait on the judgment of fairies!"

"What do you mean, 'the judgment of fairies'?" asked Ruby and Martha at the same time, getting on their feet.

"Do you think the fairies won't have a say in all of this? This is their perfect opportunity to put us on trial, while we're trapped here in this place. Gods, they've been threatening to for ages! And now that Circe is their creature, we won't have her to defend us. We'll need to defend ourselves! We need to be ready!"

Ruby and Martha looked at Lucinda, tears

welling up in their bug eyes. "Circe isn't the fairies' creature!"

"Of course she is!" spat Lucinda. "She's turned against us for the love of Nanny and her horrible sister, the Fairy Godmother. They've asked her to be an honorary wish-granting fairy. Our Circe, an honorary fairy! After everything they did to Maleficent? How could Circe even conceive of the idea? She is a witch! Honored by the gods and conceived of the three. There is no way I will let her be tainted by the fairies. And there is no way I will allow them to use our daughter while they sit in judgment of us. I can't believe you would be content in just waiting! Waiting? Have you lost all your senses? What has happened to you, my sisters?" Ruby and Martha looked at Lucinda sheepishly, finally answering.

"*You* happened to us!"

"What madness is this? What have I done?"

"You told us we must try to be better witches for Circe. Now you want to kill everyone she loves!" Ruby said.

Martha chimed in. "You insisted we speak properly, stop meddling, and make all our decisions with Circe in mind."

Ruby took over again. "You said making her happy would be the only way to get her back, Lucinda! And we want her back! We want her back!"

Martha joined her sister's chant. "We want her back!" Ruby and Martha stamped their feet, spinning in circles, and ripped at their tattered blood-stained dresses, their voices growing louder with every revolution. "We want her back! We want her back!"

Lucinda stood twitching before her sisters. "Stop this at once! I won't have these theatrics!" She stood there, looking at her hysterical sisters in their ruined dresses, tattered and torn, barely clinging their thin, frail bodies. She didn't even have the power to give them something decent to wear. Even the most mundane non-magical person in the dreamscape had the power to change their clothing, but Circe had taken everything from them. Including their dignity.

Still, Lucinda knew her sisters were right. She *had* said those things. How was she going to make Ruby and Martha understand it was time to change their methods? Time to be the powerful witches they were? At long last, it was time to leave the dreamscape and reclaim their rightful place in their own lands. But Lucinda wasn't sure her sisters were ready to hear the truth, so she kept it to herself. Her sisters had always been fragile, but she feared for their sanity now more than ever.

She had been keeping a secret from them for their entire lives. To tell them now would almost surely mean disaster. It was a secret she hoped even Circe wouldn't learn. As much as she loved her sisters, she knew their wills were too weak to keep something like this to themselves. Oh, they knew part of the story. But they didn't know the most important part, and it could destroy them all if Circe found out. And that was why more than anything they needed to get out of this place. They needed to destroy Gothel's library.

"Sisters, listen, I am the eldest. I need you to trust that I know best."

Her two sisters started to laugh. "Oh, Lucinda knows best!" cackled Ruby and Martha. "Lucinda knows best! Did you hear that?"

"Sisters, please. Use all your will and try to listen to me! This is important!" But Ruby and Martha kept mocking their sister with their chant.

"Lucinda knows best, Lucinda knows best!" Without her magic, Lucinda was forced to put her hands on her sisters, taking each of them firmly by the neck and lifting them off their feet to dangle like helpless rag dolls.

"You will stop this at once and listen to me!" The room started to rattle and shake, causing the mirrors to vibrate and bow until they nearly shattered. Lucinda released her sisters to the ground, where Martha clung to Ruby in fear.

"What's happening? Lucinda, stop! We will listen to you!"

"Oh, Lucinda, we are sorry! Please stop this!"

Lucinda went rigid, silently considering the room. Considering the mirrors. Something was wrong. She searched each mirror for the witch she was certain lurked behind one of them.

The room continued to shake. "Lucinda, please!" Ruby and Martha clung to each other. "We promise to do whatever you say! Don't break our mirrors, it's all we have!"

"This isn't my magic, you fools. We have no magic here! Now get back! Behind me, now!" Lucinda pushed her sisters behind her and stretched out her arms.

She hissed, "Reveal yourself now, witch!"

The mirrors in the chamber trembled, filling with green flames.

"It's Maleficent!" screamed Ruby. "She's back! She's found her way out of the darkness! She's crossed the veil without our help! Oh, I knew she was strong!"

The flames grew, so bright and hot they seemed about to jump out of the mirrors and into the room itself. Then a face appeared from the flames, reflected in every surface. It was pale, with large beautiful dark eyes. She looked exactly as the odd sisters remembered her so many years earlier.

It wasn't Maleficent.

"It's Grimhilde!" the three sisters said at once.

"Hello, foul witches." Her voice echoed from every mirror in the chamber. Ruby and Martha spun in circles, trying to figure out which of the many reflections was the real Grimhilde and which were illusions.

"Sisters! She is there," Lucinda said, pointing at the mirror directly in front of them. The old queen Grimhilde looked more striking than Lucinda remembered.

Cold. Steely. Beautiful.

Lucinda wondered if trapping her within the mirror like they had done to her father before her was a punishment at all. Now she was eternally young and beautiful, and somehow stronger than Lucinda remembered her.

"How did you get into the dreamscape?" Lucinda's question made Grimhilde laugh.

"It's your magic, Lucinda. You cast the spell that trapped me in the world of mirrors. And yet you don't know how I am able to appear before you?" Lucinda wondered if Grimhilde would work out that she was no longer bound by their spell. She suddenly felt self-conscious, standing before the queen in her tattered, bloodstained clothing. How she wished she wasn't trapped in the dreamscape, powerless with only her witless sisters. She longed to be in their own lands, where they would rule as queens. Instead she was in the land of mirrors and madness, talking to the old queen Grimhilde. What did the queen think of them, trapped in this place, so frightful-looking?

Curse Circe for taking away our powers! We're help-less without them and our mirrors!

Then, as she realized something, she laughed.

"The mirrors! Circe, the smartest, most powerful witch of any age forgot to enchant the dreamscape's mirrors so that Grimhilde couldn't enter!" Lucinda's laugh echoed throughout the chamber.

The wicked queen narrowed her eyes at Lucinda.

"Aren't you the least bit interested in knowing why I've come here, or are you content to stand there and laugh until I get bored and walk away?"

"Oh, I know exactly why you're here, witch. You're here for revenge."

Ruby and Martha screamed. "It's not fair! We don't have our powers! We have no means to defend ourselves! It isn't fair! It isn't fair!"

Grimhilde shook her head. "Calm yourselves. I'm not going to hurt you, though by rights I should. I'm here because I need your help."

The sisters were silenced. Their eyes bulged with shock. They didn't know how to respond. They just stood there, twitching and sputtering, the three of them thunderstruck.

"Clearly I've made a mistake coming here. You're even more insane than the last time I saw you." Grimhilde chuckled and continued. "Even if I was here for revenge, I wouldn't be able to bring myself to wield my magic against you. Not as you are now. Defenseless, forgotten, and addled. You're pathetic."

"How dare you—"

Grimhilde cut her off. "How dare I? How dare *you*? You destroyed my life! You contrived to have me kill my own daughter! And now *your* daughter, your Circe, has taken Snow from me! My poor Snow, whose nightmares are still filled with visions of you! I should destroy you where you stand!" The witch's eyes were conflicted. "But I came to you for help. After everything Maleficent told me about you, I thought—well, it doesn't matter what I thought. I see I've made a mistake coming here. You are losing your minds. I dare say they are already lost! Any revenge I could take on you would be nothing compared to the torment you're suffering here, trapped without your daughter in this perpetual madness. It's exactly what you deserve."

Grimhilde turned away, moving farther into the depths of the mirror, where she almost disappeared into the flickering green flames.

"No! Grimhilde, wait!"

"Yes, Lucinda?" The wicked queen paused and glanced back over her shoulder.

28

"What do you want of us?"

The queen sighed. She seemed to make a decision and turned back to the sisters.

"I want you to help me get Snow White back. I want a spell to bind her to me. I'm willing to do anything in exchange." Lucinda could see that Grimhilde was being honest. She sensed her desperation. She felt it almost as acutely as her own longing for Circe.

"I see," said Lucinda. "And where is your daughter now?"

"She is with Circe, among the fairies."

"Oh, is she? Well, we have a plan for the fairies," said Lucinda, her voice calm and steady.

"One that you can wield from the dreamscape?" Grimhilde asked, a hint of irony in her voice as she looked around the small room.

"With your help," Lucinda said, smiling.

"And you promise my daughter won't be harmed."

"We promise no harm will come to your *daughter*."

"Are you willing to be bound by those words, by blood, and by magic?" the old queen asked, looking at them through narrowed eyes, as if it would help her see whether they were telling the truth. Lucinda smiled at her sisters, who smiled back at her in agreement. "We will happily bind ourselves to that oath."

"Then tell me what you need me to do!"

"We need you to find one of Maleficent's birds," said Lucinda.

"I think I can do that," said Grimhilde with a wicked grin the odd sisters recognized. It was the same grin they'd seen on her face after she had drunk the potion they had given her years before—on the day she ordered the huntsman to murder Snow White. Lucinda was pleased to see Grimhilde hadn't lost her hate; it was blazing inside her like the fires of Hades.

Lucinda didn't know if she could trust Grimhilde, but perhaps coming together would bring them the one thing they both desired even more than revenge.

Their daughters.

Chapter II

After the End

Snow White and Circe had been reading the book of fairy tales while they were traveling in the odd sisters' house. They had been trapped there since the house took them to its place of origin, a place known as the Beginning.

Much of the lore surrounding the odd sisters' house was a mystery. There were secrets hidden within its walls and its bookshelves and steeped in its very being. One such secret was where the house had been created. The odd sisters had introduced a fail-safe when the house was first built. Should anything ever happen to them, the house would take its inhabitants to its place of birth. The sisters wanted to be sure their secrets would be safe should they ever be compromised while away from their home.

And that was exactly what happened: Circe and Show White were inside the house when the odd sisters went to the dreamscape, and the house took them to a place outside the many kingdoms.

The Beginning was a celestial landscape filled with stars and swirling constellations. They were trapped and had no idea where they were or how to escape. So they occupied themselves by reading the book of fairy tales and the odd sisters' journals. They thought perhaps they would find answers in the journals that would lead them back home. They were so worried about everyone in Morningstar Kingdom after their battle with Maleficent. But soon they became distracted by reading Gothel's story in the book of fairy tales. They couldn't believe how deeply the odd sisters were involved.

Circe was so angry with her mothers she took away their powers.

And then, without explanation, the house released them from the Beginning.

With the sudden freedom to travel where their hearts led them, Circe and Snow White wanted to make sure everyone they had read about in Gothel's story was safe.

First their journey took them to Rapunzel, where they saw her happy ending with their own eyes. Then they traveled to check on Mrs. Tiddlebottom, a dear old woman who had cared for Rapunzel when she was very young and who now looked after the bodies of Gothel's sisters, Hazel and Primrose. Once satisfied everyone in Gothel's story was safe, Circe and Snow headed back to Morningstar Kingdom in the aftermath of their battle with Maleficent to see how Nanny, Tulip, and Oberon were faring.

Even though what they had learned from reading Gothel's story in the book of fairy tales was still very much on their minds, their hearts were in Morningstar. As Circe and Snow White traveled, they read the ending of Maleficent's story again just as they were starting their own adventure.

✤ ✤ ✤ ✤

Nanny stood among the ruins of Morningstar Castle. The Fairy Godmother had sent the good fairies off to help Prince Phillip fight the dragon and stayed behind to help her sister repair the damages to Morningstar and to tend to everyone's injuries after the terrible battle with Maleficent.

"Thank you for your help, Sister," Nanny said sincerely.

The Fairy Godmother kissed her sister on the cheek. "It's my pleasure, dear. We have repaired far worse in our time, you and I. I'm just happy no one in the castle was seriously hurt." Nanny looked around, trying to find Tulip. "Are you looking for Princess Tulip?" the Fairy Godmother asked. "She is with Popinjay. They are doing what they can to help Oberon's army. He lost many friends in his battle with Maleficent."

Nanny was heartbroken. Everything had turned to ruins, and the Fairy Godmother could see the pain in her sister's face. "Don't fret, my dear. You really did all you could for Maleficent. I'm just sorry I never helped you. Perhaps if I had . . ."

Nanny hugged her sister. "Let's not speak of it now.

I know your heart. I know." And she cried. She cried harder than she ever had. She had lost so much. She'd lost Maleficent, and she didn't know how to find Circe, who was traveling to places unknown in the odd sisters' magical house.

"You have me. You will always have me," her sister reminded her. "Speak to Pflanze. She likely knows more about the lore surrounding the odd sisters' house than anyone. I'm sure Circe and Snow will find their way back safely before we know it."

"You're probably right, Sister. I'd better go help Tulip with the Tree Lords. Perhaps I can heal them with my magic," Nanny said, still looking very concerned.

The Fairy Godmother thought that was a good plan. "I'll stay here and repair the castle . . ." And before she could finish her thought, a magnificent dragonfly appeared with a message from the Fairylands.

"What's this?" The Fairy Godmother opened the scroll and read it. "It's from Merryweather. She says Aurora has woken up. Prince Phillip has broken the curse." She looked at her sister, knowing the good news also brought heartache.

Nanny shook her head. "No, I'm happy for the princess, and for King Stephan's court. I'm sure the good news has brought love and light to everyone in the kingdom, and I'm so glad the princess will be happy. She deserves that."

The Fairy Godmother took her sister into her arms. "And in a way, Maleficent is finally happy. She lives on in her daughter, Aurora."

Nanny thought her sister was right. That, at least, gave Nanny peace. For now. Until she turned her mind to other matters. But in that moment, she would be happy the princess lived to find true love with her prince. And Nanny was comforted in the knowledge that Maleficent would, in some fashion, live on in Aurora.

Even if the histories and books of fairy tales left that part out, she knew. And that was all that mattered.

⚜ ⚜ ⚜ ⚜

"Snow, stop reading," said Circe. "It's breaking my heart. Besides, we're almost there." Circe looked out the window of her mothers' cottage as it flew through the air. "Look, I can see Morningstar." Snow put down the book of fairy tales and looked up excitedly.

"Oh! Are we? Nanny will be so happy to see you."

Circe perched her mothers' house on the black rocky cliffs that overlooked what had once been the domain of the sea witch, Ursula. The view of Morningstar Castle from the large round kitchen window was a startling sight. Though the Lighthouse of the Gods stood untouched by the great war between Maleficent and the Tree Lords, the castle was still in disrepair. The battlements that faced the cliffs were crumbled, lying in heaps at the base of the castle like broken Cyclopean tombstones. Two of the towers were completely destroyed, including the one that had held Tulip's chambers. The sight sent chills through Circe's heart.

"Well," Circe said quietly, taking in the damage as she prepared some tea for her cousin, "at least we were expecting it. And Nanny said Tulip was safe, right?"

Snow White was sitting on a little red velvet love seat with a heap of letters on her lap, looking out the large round window. "Nanny's letters and the book of fairy tales say Tulip is well, and that she and the Fairy Godmother are working to repair the damage to the castle." Circe looked up from the tray of tea and cakes she held and smiled at her cousin.

"Thank you for going through all those letters and books. Are you sure you wouldn't be more comfortable at home in your own castle?"

"Are you trying to get rid of me already?" Snow said, winking at her cousin.

Circe set down the tray on the little table and rushed over to Snow. "Of course not! I'm so happy you're here! But I'm worried you will be bored sequestered in the house while I'm at the castle. I know it may seem overprotective, but Nanny really does feel you'd be safer here than at the castle, with my mothers' bodies still in the solarium."

Snow smiled. "I understand. I have the fairy tale book and all these letters to keep me occupied. Besides, I'm not at all ready to go back to my old life. Not just yet."

Snow laughed at the stack of letters. "That poor little owl. Nanny must have kept him busy while she was unable to reach us. By the look of it, she sent several letters a day while we were in that strange and beautiful place."

"The Beginning," Circe reminded her. "There's so much I don't know about my mothers, or this house. I wonder if the fail-safe spell was reversed when I took away their powers."

Snow White smiled at Circe. "Well, that is why I am here, to help you in your research. You haven't even had time to process everything that happened to Gothel, let alone Maleficent. There are some things your mothers said that I'm finding really curious, and I want to know more. And I know you want nothing more than to go through all these books, but you can't be in two places at once. At least, I don't think you can," Snow said, giving Circe a playful look. "So please let me help you. I'm happy to do it, truly I am."

Circe poured her cousin a cup of tea and watched

her take a sip. "You know, that cup used to be yours. I read it in Lucinda's journal," Circe said.

Snow looked at it closely and smiled. "I thought so! I'm guessing your sisters—I mean, *mothers*—took it from my parents all those years ago?"

Circe nodded. "I'm still trying to figure out what they were doing with all these cups. Do you think they could just be mementos of their misdeeds, or is there something more sinister at work?"

"I think I read something about the cups in Maleficent's story, actually. Do you want me to—" Before Snow could finish, Circe snatched the cup from her and threw it across the room. It shattered against the wall.

"Circe!" Snow was shocked. "Circe, please calm down!"

Circe took Snow by the hands, clenching them tightly. "Oh, my goodness, I am so sorry, Snow. I don't know what came over me. I think I'm much angrier with my mothers than I realized."

"I understand, sweet Circe, I do. But please, go see Nanny, she's been so worried about you, and I think it will do you good to see her. I promise I will be fine here. I want to read the rest of the fairy tale book in peace."

"You're right. I'm sorry. I think seeing Nanny will help." Circe put her hand on Snow's cheek. "My dearest Snow, should I have taken you home after we checked on Mrs. Tiddlebottom and her charges? Have I asked too much of you? Won't your husband be worried?"

Snow White kissed Circe on the cheek. "No, Circe. My dear, sweet husband understands. He's never been comfortable with how close I am with my mother, and I think he is happy that I am finding my independence without her."

Circe was happy to hear that. "I'm going to enchant the house while I'm at the castle, Snow. No one will be able to enter. I promise, you will be safe. And if you need me, for anything at all, you can contact me through the hand mirror." She paused, worried. "You're sure you will be okay here alone? Maybe I should try to convince Nanny it's okay for you to come with me to the castle."

Snow shook her head. "No. I understand completely. Really. Nanny thinks I will be safer here. I get it, Circe. Please don't worry."

Circe smiled at her cousin again. She thought Snow had such a beautiful soul. Who else would have dropped her entire life to go on this adventure with her? Who else would have ventured to distant lands to check on the sisters of a terrible witch who kidnapped children, or seen to a sweet, befuddled elderly woman consumed with baking birthday cakes? Even though Snow was much older than Circe, it sometimes seemed that she was just a little girl. There was a youthfulness about her that Circe found utterly charming. A kindness she felt she didn't deserve, not after everything her mothers had done to Snow years ago. Snow had proven that she was a wonderful woman with a forgiving heart. A woman who could forgive even her own mother for trying to kill her.

"You know, Snow, I truly love you," said Circe.

"And I love you, too, Circe."

The ladies hugged and hugged. Circe didn't want to leave Snow. "And if you learn anything important in the fairy tale book, you'll let me know?"

Snow had the book in her hand. She looked down at it. "Of course I will. Now go and give my regards to Nanny."

With a kiss for Snow and a protective enchantment on the house, Circe left for the castle.

✤ ✤ ✤ ✤

As she traveled, Circe couldn't help feeling that her heart was still with Snow. She looked back at her mothers' house, silhouetted against the crashing waves. With its witch's-cap roof, dark green hue, and black shutters, it was the last place you would expect Snow White to live. Circe laughed, lost in her thoughts and the beauty of the landscape. She had missed Morningstar, with its brilliant lighthouse and glittering sea. Then, as she neared the castle and her heart skipped a beat, Circe could see Nanny and her sister, the Fairy Godmother, in the distance outside the gates. They looked like they were talking about something important. She sped up her pace, but a voice she hadn't expected to hear startled her.

Hello, Circe. Circe spun around, wondering where the voice had come from. Then something soft brushed against her legs.

It was Pflanze. The odd sisters' cat was a tortoiseshell telepathic beauty with orange, black, and white markings.

"Pflanze!" Circe squealed with delight, though it seemed Pflanze wasn't as happy to see Circe. She just looked up at Circe with narrowed eyes, shifting her weight from one marshmallow-white paw to the other.

As long as Circe could remember, Pflanze had always been there. When Circe was younger, the cat had almost been like another sister. The most levelheaded sister in the house. The wisest, and most mysterious. There was so much more to Pflanze than Circe had ever suspected. And it was all in her mothers' journals. She had always felt she and

Pflanze had an understanding. But that day something seemed different.

I'm so disappointed in you, my little one, the cat said. *But there is no time to discuss my broken heart. I must get back to your mothers. They have been waiting for you. We all have.* Pflanze gave her a disapproving look.

"I know, Pflanze, I'm sorry. I was trapped in the Beginning."

Pflanze blinked and said, *So the house took you to the place of its birth, and you took away your mothers' powers to get out?*

Circe didn't understand what the cat meant. "Of course I didn't, Pflanze! How was I to know taking away my mothers' powers would release us from the Beginning?"

So lofty Circe took away her mothers' powers for noble reasons. I see. Well, you have much more to learn. When you took away your mothers' powers, every spell they had ever cast was broken, including the fail-safe on the house. That's why you were able to return to the many kingdoms. We have so much to talk about, Circe. There's much you need to learn, and not all of it is in those journals and that fairy tale book Snow White is reading now. If your mothers knew she was in their house, touching their things . . . do you have any idea how angry they would be, Circe?

Circe was past caring what her mothers thought.

Oh, that's very nice, Circe, said Pflanze sarcastically.

Circe had always thought she and Pflanze felt the same way about Lucinda, Ruby, and Martha. Of course the cat loved them, but she remembered times when Pflanze would become so fed up with the odd sisters' theatrics that she would leave for days just to get away from them. Now it seemed Pflanze was more loyal to them than ever.

I have always been loyal to your mothers, Circe. Always. Long before you ever came into being. Don't forget that. I saw what they went through to bring you back. I saw them deteriorate into what they've become all for the love of their precious Circe. You think they've destroyed everyone in their path? You think they're foul murderous creatures? Well, I can say the same of you. You did this to them, Circe. Your life brought all of this about. If there is nothing good left within them, it's because they gave it all to you. Remember, Circe, you are them. To hurt them would be like hurting yourself.

Circe didn't know what to say. Pflanze's words wounded her deeply, threatening to break her heart into tiny pieces. It felt like one of her mothers' mirrors; with each heartbreak there was another crack in the mirror, and she wondered how long it would be before it shattered entirely. How long before it sliced at her insides like Grimhilde once described in the book of fairy tales.

"Do you know why they hate Snow White?" she asked.

Pflanze adjusted her paws, giving Circe one of her characteristic looks. Circe could feel that Pflanze was surprised she hadn't worked it out on her own.

It was never really about Grimhilde, not until she had your mothers escorted out of the solstice celebration, humiliating them in front of the entire court. That is when their hate switched from Snow White to Grimhilde. They always hated the little brat.

"Don't call her that!"

Pflanze saw beyond Circe's anger. She saw into her heart.

You have no idea why your mothers wanted to get rid of Snow White! Why they still want to see her dead. What did you do the entire time you were trapped in the Beginning, if not read your mothers' journals? You know nothing of the women you've condemned to solitude.

"Would you like to come with me to the castle, Pflanze?"

Pflanze didn't answer. Her silence stung Circe's heart.

"And where are my mothers' bodies? Are you so angry with me that you've left them alone and defenseless in the solarium so you could condemn me?"

Pflanze didn't answer.

"Never mind. But don't think this conversation is over."

Oh, I think it is. If you want to know why your mothers hate Snow White, tell the brat queen to look it up in your mothers' journals. I imagine she will find it in the section devoted to Grimhilde. I suppose you have one of your mothers' mirrors in your pocket so you can contact the brat queen?

"I do."

I see. So you're not opposed to using your mothers' magic when it suits you. You think you're helping Snow White by keeping her locked away in their house? Leaving her alone with only a mirror for comfort and communication? Doesn't that sound like the life you are trying to save her from?

Pflanze ran ahead before Circe could answer, leaving her feeling desperately sad and alone. She had always thought she could count on Pflanze, but it was clear something within the cat had changed.

Circe missed Snow. They had been together in her mothers' house since it spirited them off to the Beginning. It felt like a lifetime, but it had all happened in a matter of days. She had felt so far away from Morningstar, and from Tulip and Nanny, when she was only reading about them rather than being there to help them during the crisis caused by her mothers. And in that moment Circe realized how much she missed and depended on Nanny. How much she loved her. She felt terrible for leaving her alone to deal with all of this, and she couldn't bear to have Nanny upset with her. She saw her in the distance, and her heart desperately wanted to be with Nanny's.

And before she understood what happened, she found herself magically transported into Nanny's arms and showered with love and affection.

"Oh, my dear sweet girl, I am so sorry I hurt your feelings when I thought you would be better off if your mothers stayed in the dreamscape. You know I only wished to protect you!" said Nanny with tears in her eyes, kissing Circe again and again, holding her face between her unbelievably soft hands.

"I'm sorry, too! I'm sorry I left you alone, Nanny. I see things much more clearly now. I know something has to be done about my mothers. I know you were only worried about me! I'm so sorry I stormed out like that, leaving you on your own to deal with Maleficent. Can you ever forgive me?"

Nanny looked into Circe's sad eyes. "Oh, my

darling girl, there is nothing to forgive. The house took you away. You didn't choose to leave. More importantly, what is this delightful advancement in your abilities?"

"What do you mean, did I teleport?" Circe asked, noticing the concerned look on Nanny's face. "I thought *you* brought me here from across the field."

Nanny shook her head. "No, my dear, that was entirely your doing. And I don't think it was teleportation."

Circe blinked, confused. But all she could think about now was how happy she was to see her dearest Nanny, who never seemed to change. Even in the wake of the Dark Fairy's death and the near destruction of Morningstar Castle, her eyes sparkled with life and love for Circe. "Oh, my dear, I'm so happy you're here. I want to hear all about your adventures with Snow White, and what you learned when you read Gothel's story," said Nanny, but before Circe could answer, they were distracted by the Fairy Godmother, screeching in the distance.

"Sister! Sister!" she cried in distress. "We have to go! We have to go!"

The Fairy Godmother wobbled toward them, completely discombobulated. She took several steps in one direction, changed her mind, and then went off in the other direction, back and forth.

"Is she okay? What's happened?"

Nanny and Circe hurried to the garden, where the Fairy Godmother was shaking and fumbling with a letter she had just read. "Sister! What's the matter?" Nanny asked.

The Fairy Godmother looked up, her face filled with terror. "Oberon says we have reason to believe the odd sisters are trying to lure Maleficent from the other side of the veil to fight at their side."

Circe felt her heart seize with panic. "Can they do that? Do they have the power to bring people back from the dead like that?"

Nanny frowned. "I don't know, my dear. I don't know. They may."

The Fairy Godmother seemed to notice Circe for the first time. "Oh! Circe, my dear. I'm so happy you're safe! You poor sweet thing! Everything you've gone through!" Circe was enveloped in the Fairy Godmother's arms. She hadn't expected her embrace to feel so much like Nanny's. To feel comforted and loved in the same way. She suddenly felt overwhelmed. Lucinda, Ruby, and Martha had always loved her. Loved her desperately. Loved her too much. This love, the love she felt from Nanny and her sister, was something quite different. It was pure. It wasn't tainted by sacrifice, the insatiable need to protect her at any cost. And Circe wondered if she was worthy of it.

"Come on, my dear. Let's go sit down," Nanny said, leading Circe to the garden outside the conservatory. The conservatory was an architectural marvel of windows and a giant domed ceiling. Large French doors led to a lush garden filled with wandering roses, wisteria, honeysuckle, and jasmine. The scent was so sweet it made Circe's head swim.

Once in the garden, they made themselves comfortable under a large blossoming tree filled with delicate pink and blue flowers. "I don't remember the tree being these colors," Circe mused. "Weren't the flowers white?"

Nanny laughed and rolled her eyes. "This is the three good fairies' handiwork. They came back to help after Aurora's wedding."

"Oh, are they still here?" Circe asked, squinting and looking around the garden for them. She didn't know how she felt having so many fairies about. It was strange enough being in the Fairy Godmother's company. Maleficent's death was still so fresh. Snow was right. She hadn't had time to properly process everything that had happened. Circe felt conflicted about the fairies. If they hadn't been so cruel to Maleficent, she might never have destroyed the Fairylands and been forced to turn to the odd sisters for help. She would never have created Aurora and lost herself in the process. And Circe's mothers—her meddlesome mothers—if they hadn't manipulated and used Gothel, then Gothel would probably be ruling the dead woods with her sisters now. So many things would be different.

My darling, it's so much more complicated than

that. Quiet your mind. Don't dwell on what might have been.

Nanny patted Circe's hand tenderly. "The three good fairies are with Tulip, Oberon, and the Tree Lords, doing their best to heal the wounded." Nanny was eyeing her sister and Circe, clearly worried about both of them. Circe had so many questions and there was so much to say, but they were being dragged into yet another of her mothers' dramas, and she felt she'd better find out what was really going on before the Fairy Godmother fretted herself into another tizzy. "Perhaps we check in on your mothers in the dreamscape? See what they're up to?" asked Nanny. Circe took her hand mirror from her pocket. She dreaded seeing them just then. But if they were planning to try to lure Maleficent from beyond the veil, that would help her in her decision. She'd been looking the other way for far too long when it came to her mothers. And it was time to put a stop to their antics and skullduggery.

"Show me the odd sisters." Circe spoke and the words caught in her rapid breath.

Rather than showing the odd sisters, the mirror filled with familiar green flames.

"Do you think your mothers succeeded in bringing her back?" Nanny's face was filled with worry. *I will never forgive my mothers if they drag that poor creature back from death. It will break Nanny's heart,* thought Circe, grasping the mirror so hard it might have broken.

"Maleficent," Circe asked, her voice shaking, "is that you?"

"No." A familiar pale face with large dark eyes appeared in the flames. "I have not seen the Dark Fairy in the world of mirrors. I believe she has passed beyond the veil."

"Grimhilde!" Nanny snatched the mirror from Circe's shaking hand. "What do you want, *witch*?"

"My daughter, of course. I'm giving you one day to return her to me. If she isn't back home safely within her own castle by this time tomorrow, you will suffer the consequences."

"Snow will never forgive you if you do this," whispered Circe.

"How dare you speak for my daughter, you spawn of guile, insanity, wretchedness! Listen to me well: I will rain terror upon your heads if my daughter is not returned to me. You have until tomorrow!"

The wicked queen's face disappeared into the green mists, leaving the ladies awestruck and afraid.

CHAPTER III

THE SINS OF OUR MOTHERS

Snow had been reading the book of fairy tales since Circe left for the castle, so she decided to take a break and make some tea. She had been rereading Gothel's story, going over some of the things the odd sisters had said that she found intriguing. Things they had said to Gothel about her mother, Manea. There seemed to be more behind their words, which often seemed to be the case with the odd sisters, but something about what Lucinda had said to Gothel in her last days resonated in Snow, and she felt there was a mystery to be solved. Her eyes were tired from long hours of reading, and she squinted at the sun coming through the round kitchen window that overlooked the apple tree. She wondered if it was the same apple tree from which her mother had plucked the apple that put her to sleep so many years before.

Snow White.

In a bit of a panic, Snow spun around, looking for the source of the otherworldly voice. Could she have summoned her mother by simply thinking of her? She suddenly felt very afraid of her mother. She felt like a young girl again. Afraid and alone.

"Mother?"

No, Snow, it's me, Circe. Snow's heart slowed.

Snow looked around the room for the origin of Circe's voice. And then she found it. Her cousin's sweet face appeared in the mirror sitting on the kitchen table.

"Oh, there you are! Is everything all right?" Snow asked, picking it up.

Yes, dear. Everything is fine. I'm just checking in to see how you're doing.

"I'm fine, Circe, really. What's going on? I can see something is bothering you."

So you've not heard from your mother? You looked frightened, Snow. What's happened?

"It's nothing, Circe, really. What's this about Mother? Has she done something?"

No, dear. I just . . . I thought I heard you mention her. Don't worry about it. I'm sorry to bother you, we have a situation here and it's got me all muddled.

"You're not a bother, Circe. What's the situation? Has it to do with my mother?"

No.

Snow could see Circe was keeping something from her. "Circe, you know I love you, but you can't keep treating me like a child who needs to be protected. That's how my mother treats me. Now, please, tell me what's going on."

Circe sighed. "We received word that my mothers may be soliciting help to break them out of the dreamscape, and I'm worried, that's all."

Snow White felt as if she might faint. She put her hand on the table to steady herself and sat down in a chair. "How? How will they break out?" She could see Circe looked concerned.

"Oberon didn't say. We're trying to get more information. But, Snow, I promise you're safe. We don't even know if that's the plan. They may just be trying to use powerful witches to do their bidding from the dreamscape. We're not sure."

Snow White could tell Circe was leaving something out. "But who? Who will they use? My mother?" Circe's expression changed.

"I doubt Grimhilde would ever help my mothers. No, the fairies received word they were trying to lure Maleficent back from the other side of the veil to fight at their side against the fairies. They think they will try to bring her back to the living."

Snow White felt the strangest sensation. A sense that what Circe was saying was not only true, but possible. "Circe, since we read Gothel's story, I've had a feeling, a suspicion I haven't shared with you."

Circe looked back at Snow in the mirror. "What is it? Why haven't you told me yet?"

"Hold on, let me go get the book of fairy tales, it's something I read in Gothel's story." Snow stood up, placing the mirror on the table. She retrieved the book and brought it back, opening to the page she had been reading earlier. But the page looked different. Snow gasped and held it to the mirror so that Circe could see.

Now there was only a single line, which read *This story is still being written.*

"The page I was looking for isn't there!" she said, shifting the mirror so she could see Circe's reaction. "It's gone, replaced by this one line! What do you think it means?"

Snow could see Circe didn't know, and she didn't want to distract her with all her theories while Circe was dealing with the debacle of her mothers. She suddenly felt foolish for bringing it up and vowed to handle it on her own. "Circe, don't worry. I will find the pages with the part of the story I was looking for, and when I have the information, I will share it with you. Now go, I'm sure Nanny and the Fairy Godmother are in a state."

Circe sighed. "Yes, we have to figure out what to do about my mothers. And the last thing Nanny needs is another fight with her adopted daughter,

Maleficent. If it's true my mothers are planning to bring her back, I will never forgive them. This is just all so heartbreaking."

Snow White nodded. "Go, Circe, and take care. I'll be fine here. I have a lot of reading to do."

Circe smiled at her cousin. "Thank you, sweet Snow. I love you."

Snow could see how upset Circe was. "I love you, too, Circe. I'll let you know if I learn anything."

But Snow White knew she probably wouldn't tell Circe. She didn't want to burden her with more wild notions about the odd sisters until she was sure.

And besides, she didn't think she would find anything just yet, not until she visited Gothel's old library. She wished she had thought of it when they went to check on Mrs. Tiddlebottom before coming back to Morningstar. She supposed she would have to invent a reason to go back there on her own.

CHAPTER IV

A FAIRY'S DUTY

Circe found Nanny and the Fairy Godmother sitting down to a pot of tea in the beautiful sunlit morning room. The large glass double doors were open to the garden, which was in full bloom. Nanny looked up from her conversation with her sister when Circe walked in.

"Circe, did you speak to Snow? Has her mother tried contacting her?"

"No, I don't think she can. I enchanted the house so no one can come in—even through the mirrors. Except for me." Circe sat down and helped herself to the tea and cakes that sat there, untouched. Both fairies looked distressed, their brows furrowed in exactly the same fashion, and for the first time, Circe noticed the similarities between the sisters. They didn't look like sisters, really, but they acted like sisters, and they shared some of the same mannerisms. But there was something more. Circe couldn't explain it. There was a bond between them Circe hadn't noticed before. A bond surely formed in the wake of Maleficent's death.

"Did you tell her she should go back to her own kingdom?" asked Nanny as Circe poured tea into the delicate rose-patterned teacups. Circe shook her head. The truth was that Circe had been tempted to, but she just couldn't bring herself to send Snow back to her old life. Not until Snow was ready. She wanted her to face her possessive mother a stronger woman. And now more than ever she wanted to keep her close, since she knew her mothers' hatred had originally been directed at Snow before Grimhilde diverted their attentions.

"I knew it was a terrible idea, bringing that girl

here," said Nanny, her hand shaking, spilling her tea all over the tablecloth.

"She isn't a girl, she's a grown woman! And what would you have me do? Ship her off to her horrible mother? Doom her to spending her days endlessly consoling her mother for trying to kill her as a child? That is not a life!" Circe could see Nanny was upset, so she reined in her anger. "Nanny, I'm sorry, I couldn't bring myself to tell Snow her mother threatened us. She would have insisted on leaving right away," she said, looking at Nanny and realizing she was more than upset. "Nanny, are you all right? When was the last time you slept or ate something? Your hands are shaking."

Nanny patted Circe's hand tenderly. Her powdery soft skin felt like thin vellum to Circe. She seemed much more delicate to Circe now, almost fragile, and it made Circe worry to see Nanny so exhausted. She wanted to bundle her up right then and there, tuck her into a cozy bed, and surround her with soft pillows. She was tempted to put a sleeping spell on her, just so the old woman could get some rest. So she could dream and be at peace.

"The last thing I need is to be trapped in the land of dreams with your mothers, Circe. The queen Grimhilde will move heaven and earth to get her daughter back, and if your mothers do manage to bring Maleficent back, you need my help," said Nanny wearily.

"What do you mean trapped with the odd sisters? Who said anything about sending you there?" The Fairy Godmother was beside herself.

"No, dear. I'm sorry. I forget you can't read minds. Circe thinks I could do with an enchanted sleep."

The Fairy Godmother yawned. "Well, I think we all could, what with dragons attacking the castle, and the ghost of Grimhilde threatening us! You know who we have to blame for this, don't you?" The Fairy Godmother gave Circe an apologetic smile and continued. "I'm sorry to say it, dear, but this is all your mothers' fault! I daresay they won't ever be getting out of the dreamscape, not if we can help it!"

The Fairy Godmother stood up on wobbly legs and tottered over to Circe, then snatched the enchanted mirror from her hands and muttered apologies. "I'm sorry, my dear. Now, please, if you don't mind, we should try to find your mothers before they raise everyone they've murdered from the dead and turn them against us!"

Circe rolled her eyes. "That's a bit dramatic, don't you think? My mothers don't have the power to raise the dead! Certainly not Ursula. Maleficent, maybe, since she just passed." Circe doubted her own words but found it hard to entertain anything the Fairy Godmother said, because she was so histrionic and set in antiquated ways.

"They trapped Grimhilde's soul in one of their magic mirrors! Who knows what other dark powers they possess? Ursula and Maleficent may swoop upon us at any moment!" Circe sighed but said nothing as she glared at the Fairy Godmother. "What? Share your thoughts!" snapped the Fairy Godmother, giving Circe a dirty look, which had until that moment been out of character for her.

"Well, if those women had had fairies to protect them, perhaps they wouldn't be dead and now at the whim of my mothers!"

The Fairy Godmother looked like she might faint at the prospect. "What in the Fairylands are you suggesting, young lady?"

Circe tried to make her voice sweet. "I'm suggesting we rethink who benefits from fairy magic. Shouldn't it be our duty to help all those in need?"

"If I recall," the Fairy Godmother said shrewdly, "you haven't yet accepted our offer to make you an honorary wish-granting fairy. And if this is the way you intend to conduct yourself in the name of the Fairylands, giving help to the likes of those horrible creatures, then I think I may reconsider the offer!" The Fairy Godmother eyed Circe reproachfully.

Just then, Tulip bounded into the morning room, all smiles. "Well, I don't know what Oberon will think of that!" she said. The Fairy Godmother flinched at Oberon's name, remembering his rebukes when he first arrived at Morningstar. Circe snickered, and then smiled at Tulip's outfit, taking delight in her suspicion that it likely scandalized the Fairy Godmother. And she was right.

"What in the Fairylands are you wearing, young lady?" Fairy Godmother was shaking with disapproval, but Tulip just laughed it off. Circe tried not to laugh, herself.

"Oh, Circe, I am so happy to see you!" The ladies kissed each other on the cheeks, laughing in their joy of reuniting—and at the Fairy Godmother's reaction, though it made them feel slightly guilty to do so.

"Tulip! Look at you. You've become quite the lady since I saw you last!" Tulip looked radiantly happy.

"I wouldn't say she looks like a lady at all!" the Fairy Godmother huffed. "Wearing trousers! It's a scandal!" Tulip just laughed again at the Fairy Godmother's fussing.

"And what would you have me wear while romping with the Tree Lords? Oberon agrees it's very sensible."

The Fairy Godmother wrinkled her nose at

Tulip. "What does your young prince think of you *romping around*, as you put it, with the Tree Lords— in trousers, no less! Shouldn't you be planning a wedding, my dear?"

Tulip gave the Fairy Godmother one of her flashing smiles, which meant she was trying not to become impatient with the meddling old woman. "Well, if you really must know, my dear sweet Popinjay also thinks my outfit is very sensible! And I have no intention of marrying him or anyone. Who has time for wedding planning when I have so much work to do with Oberon, restoring the land after it was devastated in the battle? Seriously, Fairy Godmother, don't be so old-fashioned."

Nanny smiled. "Well, don't let your mother hear you talking like that. I think she'd share my sister's opinion."

"I *know* she would!" snapped the Fairy Godmother.

Circe chimed in. "Oh, stop it, the both of you. I think Tulip looks beautiful. More importantly, she looks happy! And she's living her life as she chooses. As I always wanted for her. And I think she's right:

Oberon would approve of extending the fairies' reach beyond the princesses."

"Now look here! I won't have you all ganging up on me!" said the Fairy Godmother, looking to Nanny. "Sister, I suppose you side with your blond beauties?" she squealed.

"I'm afraid I do, Sister. You know I do! This is something I've wanted for our kind for a long time."

Circe was proud of Nanny. "I think it's time to make the decision now to help all those in need if it's within our power," she said, beaming at being supported by Nanny and Tulip.

"Something like this has to be brought to the fairy council first, Circe. But I wouldn't do anything to upset them, not right now," the Fairy Godmother said.

"And why not?" Circe asked. Nanny and the Fairy Godmother shared a look. "What? What aren't you telling me?" Circe's smile diminished.

"Circe," Nanny said gently, "there's something we have to tell you. The Council—"

"Your mothers are about to be put on trial!" the

Fairy Godmother blurted, almost happily. "The fairies are building a case against them."

"A trial? What do you mean? Shouldn't we be focusing on stopping them from escaping? Keeping them from dredging up the dead to help them in their cause?" Circe's voice rose in frustration.

"We must go about things properly, Circe! The council must weigh in. There has to be a trial before we take any further action against them. Oberon is already angry that we put your mothers to sleep without taking everything into account, and with this trial, we will," said the Fairy Godmother.

"When were you going to tell me? Was I even going to be asked to attend?"

The Fairy Godmother eyed Circe carefully. "I might have asked you, but after your remarks today, I'm not sure it's a good idea. I don't think you are impartial when it comes to your mothers."

"Now, wait, Sister. Circe is the one who took away her mothers' powers and locked them in the dreamscape. She may not be impartial, but she wants to see justice just as much as we do. We are all on the same side. And nothing will be solved if we're divided." Nanny turned to Circe. "And, my dear, as much as I don't like it, this really *should* go to trial. We all have to decide together what should be done about your mothers."

The Fairy Godmother grinned smugly. "Then it's all decided. The matter of the odd sisters will go before the fairy council."

"But someone has to find out what my mothers are really up to! Someone has to stop them! We can't waste time on this ridiculous trial when there are more immediate dangers. We all know they've done reprehensible things, we don't have to prove it." Circe was becoming even more impatient.

"You're right, my dear, we don't need to prove it. But we do need to decide what the consequences should be for the damage they've done. We must decide what should be done about them, once and for all—and keep them from ever causing this kind of destruction again." Malice twinkled in the Fairy Godmother's eye. "I'm sure the three good fairies will want to weigh in."

"Oh, I'm sure they would!" Circe was about to say something unkind. She was out of patience with the Fairy Godmother. Surely it was up to her to decide what to do about her own mothers. She didn't want the fairies to make that decision.

Nanny, who could read Circe's thoughts, took her by the hand. "Circe, my darling, please don't worry. Let me go to the Fairylands in your name while you find a way to stop your mothers. You trust me, do you not?"

Circe smiled. "Of course I trust you."

"Well, then, let me do this for you. Besides, it's been far too long since I visited the place of my birth. I might find that I feel differently about it now."

CHAPTER V

THE MOURNING BOX

Snow's mind had been flooded with questions after she read Gothel's story, so she searched through all the odd sisters' books, looking for more information about the dead woods. She wondered how it was that the odd sisters could enter the dead woods with all the enchantments Manea had placed on the boundaries. But even more distracting were some of the things Lucinda and her sisters said to Gothel. How did the odd sisters know so much about the dead woods and the witches who had lived there over the ages? How did Lucinda know things about Gothel's childhood that Gothel didn't even know?

But when Snow tried to find those sections again in the book of fairy tales, she found something much more disturbing: a story she had never read before. She curled up in her favorite red love seat with a cup of tea, hoping she would find the answers she was looking for.

The Mourning Box

Tucked snugly away, deep within the dead forest, was a family of witches.

Their cold gray cobblestone mansion was perched on the tallest hill, giving them an awe-inspiring view of the city of the dead, under the shadows of the lifeless trees, with rows of crypts and tombstones stretched for miles. An enchanted, impenetrable thicket of rosebushes circled the forest, keeping the witches in and the living out. With very few exceptions.

Two of the witches were older than either of them could recall. The third had just been born, on the day this story begins. She was the only child of Manea, who herself was the only daughter of the dreaded and fearsome Nestis—the reigning queen of the dead woods. Though there had been many ruling queens in the dead woods, Nestis was by far the nastiest and most powerful that the woods had ever produced.

But the queen of the dead showed her daughter nothing but love and prepared her for the day she would take the throne in her place—a tradition Manea herself would not embrace when she would eventually become queen of the dead. But Nestis foresaw the coming of a great and powerful witch, empowered by the blood of the witches who came before her. She saw that her daughter Manea would bring this witch into the world, and therefore treated her like the queen she would one day become. More importantly, she treated her like the mother of the most powerful queen these lands would ever see. And once her daughter had given birth to this new and powerful little witch, even though she was a gift from the gods, Nestis wanted more.

She wanted three.

"Everyone knows three identical daughters are favored by the gods, Manea," said Nestis from the throne in her bedchamber. It was large and impressive, carved from stone in the image of the giant winged beast. Nestis always seemed to be in the shadow of this dragon, its wings acting as her armrests and its head peering over her left shoulder, seeming to whisper advice in her ear. The only feature in the room that was grander was the stone bed, also decorated with carved dragons.

"I know, Mother. The gods didn't see fit to grant me three. But my daughter is a great gift. You said so yourself. She is the most powerful witch these lands have ever beheld. Can't we be contented and celebrate that?" Manea stood trembling before her mother, cold in the drafty room. Chilled to the bone by the dampness within the stone walls, daunted by the dragons that decorated it, and worried about the fate of her newborn daughter.

"And that is why I fear you are not worthy to take my place, my little one, my blackhearted child. You have no imagination. You never reach

for greatness." Nestis smirked at her daughter.

"Mother! Why am I never able to please you? I have produced the most powerful witch in our line, and still you are not satisfied." Manea's eyes were bulging; her stringy black hair was mussed and stuck to her blanched face.

"No, I am not!" said Nestis, standing up. "I want the three most powerful witches. We will split them. Tomorrow."

"Split them? What do you mean 'split them'?"

"I mean exactly that. I will make one into three." Nestis walked to her writing table and took out a piece of parchment.

"But that doesn't make sense. If you split her power among three, then won't they each be weaker and less powerful?"

"Not with my *blood within their veins, they won't. They will be the most powerful witches these lands have ever seen." Nestis scribbled a hasty note and rang the small bell that hung on the wall above her fireplace mantel.*

"She is already the most powerful! Please,

Mother, don't do this!" Manea was filled with dread at the idea of splitting her daughter. Maybe it was the word, split. *It seemed dangerous, gruesome, violent. She wouldn't have it. As she was trying to find the right argument, the right words to plead with her mother, one of her mother's skeletal servants entered the room.*

"Here, take this," Nestis said. "Bring him to me at once." With that, she dismissed the servant and turned her attention back to her daughter. Manea wondered what her mother meant, but was afraid to ask. "Their reign will be legendary. Don't you see? There won't be any need for succession after them. We can mold them in our image, teach them our traditions and our magic, and when it's our time to pass into the mists, we will know our lands will be protected. Our magic will live on in them, leaving nothing to chance."

"Mother, I'm begging you. Don't do this to my daughter!"

"Trust me, my dear. Your little beastie will be safe, I promise you. No harm will come to her. And

think how much happier you will be when you have three daughters to love and cherish. Think how favored we will be among our ancestors and the gods. There will be nothing and nowhere that won't be within our command once they are born."

"Mother! Do you mean to say you wish to extend our reign beyond the boundaries of the dead woods? No modern witch has ever crossed the boundary. And in return the living give us their dead. It has been so since before the recording of time," said Manea, shocked her mother would even attempt such a thing.

"Do not presume to tell me our history, Daughter! I have discussed it with our ancestors, and I have been given permission to cross the boundary if we succeed in the making of three."

"But this is folly, Mother! This flies in the face of our entire history, of everything we have been taught. I don't believe the ancestors have agreed to this."

"You dare question me?" Manea had never seen her mother so angry. She had never felt afraid of her

mother before, and it was an odd sensation to want to cower before her. But before she could say anything, her mother's expression changed and softened.

"This is my fault. I have given you the impression that your opinion is welcome. I have shared too much with you, my daughter, but never forget I am the queen here, and my word is paramount. Cross me again, and you will regret it. Do not invite my wrath."

"Mother, please. Surely I should have a say in what happens to my own daughter?"

"No, my dear, you do not. Go now and be with your daughter. Treasure her as one, and I hope tomorrow you will be able to treasure her as three. Because she will be three, my dear, whether you want it or not. Now leave me before I become truly angry with you."

Manea left her mother's room and went up to the nursery, her eyes filled with tears and her heart filled with dread. Her daughter was sleeping soundly in the stone-carved bird's nest nestled in the branches of a statue of a tree in the center of the room. She looked so snug, swaddled in her blankets. Gray stone ravens perched above her, looking down on the baby lovingly. The great altar at the far right of the room was covered with small paintings of the many queens who had once ruled the dead woods and who were now in the mists. Their ancestors.

Nestis was the only one who spoke with their ancestors, but Manea was in a panic. She had to know if her mother was telling her the truth. Something within her said she wasn't. The same voice that had warned her that splitting her daughter would be disastrous guided her in this moment. She opened the wooden box on the altar and lit the candle inside with trembling hands. "Honored ancestors, please forgive me for disturbing you in the mists, but I am concerned about your plans for my daughter."

An uncanny voice came out of the ether. A calming and reassuring woman's voice.

"We are very pleased with the birth of your daughter, Manea."

Manea hadn't known what to expect, though this woman's voice, this faceless ancestor, caught her off guard with how gentle and kind she sounded.

"But it is still too early to concern yourself with our plans for her. While your mother is still in power, our intentions and dreams are with her."

"Then you've not given her permission to split my daughter in three?"

"She doesn't need our permission to strengthen the line, Manea. You know this."

"But she would need your permission if she wanted to extend our reign beyond the boundaries."

"Beyond the boundaries? No witch since that of the First sought to rule outside the boundaries. What is this madness? Are you sure this is her plan?"

"She told me so just now. I don't wish to betray her, but I am so worried."

"But you have betrayed her by coming to us. Go along with your mother's plan. We promise you

we will not let it go too far. Now go, see to your little girl. You have done well, Manea. You have given our family a great gift, and we will not let your mother destroy everything we have built here."

"Bless you." And she blew out the candle and closed the lid of the wooden box. The black candle smoke spiraled up, dancing before her, and she stood almost transfixed until something outside the nursery window caught her eye.

It was Jacob. Her beloved.

Manea's heart raced when she saw him. What was he doing there?

"He's here because I asked him." Manea whipped around and saw her mother standing in the doorway.

"Mother!"

Her mother stood there, contemplating the room and searching Manea's mind for the answers she was seeking. It felt like skeletal hands clawing at Manea's brain. She could sense her mother digging around, trying to find her secrets.

"I smell candle wax and smoke. Were you speaking to our ancestors?"

"I wanted them to bless my daughter," said Manea, trembling, eyeing her daughter, who was still asleep in her nest.

"Lies!" Manea had never heard her mother scream, but before she could react, she was struck by a massive blow that sent her flying across the room and into the family altar, scattering the portraits and knocking the mourning box onto the floor.

"Ancestors, please help me!"

She reached for the wooden box, but it flew from her grasp and shattered against a stone raven, waking the baby witch.

Manea gathered all her courage, stood up slowly, and made her way to the screaming baby.

"Don't you touch her, Manea!"

Manea didn't listen; she rushed to her daughter and took her in her arms. "Hush now, my little girl. Mother is here. She loves you."

"Give the child to me!" Nestis's face mutated

in fury. Manea had never seen her like that. She looked like a wild beast, ugly and disfigured by her anger, but Manea stood her ground.

"Never! I won't let you have her!"

Nestis narrowed her eyes and became very still. Something about it sent a chill through Manea.

"Bring him!" Nestis said calmly, and Manea knew she wasn't speaking to her. Two skeletal minions brought Jacob into the nursery. He was battered, bruised, and bloody, unable to speak or walk on his own.

"Jacob, no!" The tall beautiful man stood before her, stupefied. "What have you done?" cried Manea.

"Give me your daughter, or I will kill him."

"I will never give you my daughter!"

"Is that your choice, then? You'd rather see the father of your child die than give her over to me?"

"He's not her father!" Manea lied, hoping to save him. "My daughter was born of magic, like all the daughters in the dead woods!"

Nestis laughed.

"Lies! I know everything, Manea! Are you foolish enough to think I don't know your every thought? Your every move? I know your heart, my dear, because your heart is my heart! I created my daughter with magic, as you were bound to do. I am the creator of fates! I let your dalliance with this human go because I saw the coming of a great and powerful witch. It was I who put this human in your path. I arranged that he be our man to do our bidding in the living world. It was by my grace and foresight that you fell in love with him, and I am happy to let you keep him. But listen to me well: I will not let you stand in the way of furthering your daughter's greatness, and furthering the greatness of our lands and our rule! So give me the child now or I will slit your lover's throat while you watch."

"He was not a dalliance! I love him!"

"Then save his life and give me the child!"

Manea took a deep breath and looked into Jacob's eyes. He was disoriented and could hardly stand. She wasn't sure he understood what was *happening or where he was. He was spellbound by her mother's magic. She loved him, she loved him so much, but she couldn't give up her daughter. Not even for Jacob.*

Oh my love, forgive me, she thought as she looked at him.

"My Jacob, my love, I am so sorry," she said as she closed her eyes. She knew what was coming. She tried to brace herself for it. She clutched her daughter so tightly in her arms she thought she might crush her. . . .

✣ ✣ ✣ ✣

Snow White put down the book. "Where is the rest?" The remaining pages were torn from the book of fairy tales. Snow's heart was racing. She felt like the theory that had sparked in her mind after reading Gothel's story was coming together with every new thing she read. It was like a puzzle, and each new bit of information was making her theory into a reality.

Don't jump to conclusions, Snow, she told herself. *You don't know for sure.*

She stood up and started pacing around the odd sisters' little house. It was so strange reading about Manea and Jacob. It made her heart hurt, knowing Manea witnessed her lover's death. *And what became of the child?*

But Snow thought she knew even as she asked herself. She knew who the child was, but she wanted to see those missing pages to be sure. She had to tell Circe.

Oh my gods. It all makes sense. All of it. If this is true, then . . .

She wanted to snatch the mirror up and call Circe at once. To tell her everything. But she didn't. The last thing she wanted to do was panic her. Not yet. She had to be sure. She needed the missing pages. She needed to know the entire story.

Suddenly, she felt faint. All the air seemed to leave the room at once, and she couldn't breathe. She needed to leave the house immediately, overcome by an overwhelming urge to flee. She ran to the door and opened it, and to her horror, sitting on the door-step was a large shining red apple. She screamed.

The thing looked sinister. Wicked. So much like the one her mother had given her years earlier. She slammed the door and screamed, "Show me Circe!" over and over until she heard Circe's voice coming from the mirror.

Snow! Are you okay?

"No, Circe, I'm not. Please come! I'm so afraid."

CHAPTER VI

THE BIRD
AND THE APPLE

"I don't understand! Who would do this?" Circe was angry, looking at the ominous apple, still sitting on the doorstep where Snow had left it.

"Calm down, my dear. We won't let anything happen to Snow, I promise." Nanny had taken control of the situation. They had both come down from the castle to the odd sisters' house to check on Snow. The Fairy Godmother had stayed behind to do the rest of the repairs before she and Nanny had to set off to the Fairylands to arrange the fairy council meeting.

Nanny looked around the odd sisters' house. She

101

wondered what it had been like for Circe to grow up in such a strange place, with its stained glass windows that celebrated her mothers' foul deeds. One of the windows depicted Snow White's fateful red apple, shining like a crimson beacon in the sunlight over the front door, and to its right was Ursula's golden seashell necklace sparkling in the light. And then she saw it, the one that broke her heart: a dragon, encircled by black crows and blowing green flames. Seeing it made her cheeks burn with guilt for the loss of Maleficent. Nanny looked around the room, trying to distract herself from her heartbreak. Some images were unfamiliar to her. She wondered how they were connected to the stories she knew. She recognized the pink rose as the Beast's but couldn't quite place some of the other symbols. Looking at Maleficent's stained glass window again, she remembered.

Her teacup!

"Excuse me, dears," she said, going to the kitchen. "I've always been curious about something." She poked around the odd sisters' cabinets until she found it. Her teacup. The one the sisters had taken when they visited for Maleficent's birthday and watched her take her fairy exams. "Ah! I knew it!"

Circe and Snow watched Nanny, puzzled. Why wasn't she more concerned about the mysterious apple? What was she looking for? "Nanny, what are you up to over there?" Circe asked.

Nanny spun around, her cheeks red. "I'm sorry, dears! I always wondered if your mothers took this teacup from me, and I find that they have. I think I'll take it back. For safekeeping until we know their menacing purpose."

Circe nodded. "Understandable. Please feel free," she said as she cleared her throat and looked at the apple as if to say it was more pressing than sinister teacups.

"Yes, of course you're right," Nanny said, turning her attention back to the apple. "It's harmless," she said. "I don't detect an enchantment or poison."

"Yes! I've already surmised that. But who would do this? It's frightened poor Snow to tears! And don't you suggest we send her home, Nanny! Not after this!" Circe was on the verge of tears herself.

"No, I quite agree, we need to keep her close so we can protect her."

"Am I to have no say in what happens to me?" said Snow, picking up the apple and holding it in her hand.

"Of course you do. I'm sorry, Cousin. But why did you try to leave the house? What was the matter?" Circe took Snow's hand and led her to the little red love seat so they could sit together.

"I don't know. I was reading a story in the book of fairy tales and I was suddenly overwhelmed. I can't explain it. I felt like I just had to get out. Like I could claw my way out of here if I had to. I'm sorry I've caused such a fuss."

"You're not causing a fuss, Snow! You've been cooped up in here for ages, and I shouldn't have left you alone."

"Circe, what would you think if I went to see Mrs. Tiddlebottom while you handled things here with Nanny? It *would* get me out of here, and I have been worried about her, left to manage Primrose and Hazel on her own. I'm afraid how she will feel once all of her memories come flooding back."

"What is this about?" asked Nanny.

"My mothers put a memory charm on Gothel's cook, Mrs. Tiddlebottom, and now that I've taken away my mothers' powers, most of their spells are waning. Snow is afraid Mrs. Tiddlebottom will be overwhelmed once she regains all of her memories."

Nanny thought about it, gleaning more information from Circe's and Snow's memories of their visit to Mrs. Tiddlebottom before they came to Morningstar. She also caught some of Gothel's story. "I think Snow is right. The poor woman may need someone there to help her."

Nanny eyed Snow White, wondering what she was up to. She believed Snow was worried about Mrs. Tiddlebottom and her charges, Primrose and Hazel—she could see it in her mind—but she also felt there was something more to this odd request. And she was surprised Snow was able to keep it to herself. Perhaps it was nothing more than guilt for not staying with Mrs. Tiddlebottom and Gothel's sisters longer. She knew Circe felt ashamed for leaving them alone so soon; that had been on Circe's mind. Perhaps Snow also felt ashamed. But why was she making this request now, in the middle of a crisis? Nanny didn't understand it. And then she grasped it, the real reason, hiding in the shadows of Snow's mind: something about looking for the missing pages from the book of fairy tales in Gothel's library, which was still at Mrs. Tiddlebottom's house. *Interesting.*

"I won't have you so far from us, Snow. I want you here, where we can protect you," said Circe, not reading Nanny's thoughts, focused as she was on her cousin.

"And what about Mrs. Tiddlebottom? Who will protect her?" Snow's lip started to tremble. She turned abruptly and left the room.

"Circe, go with her. You told me yourself you were worried about Primrose and Hazel," said Nanny.

"Did I?"

"Well, not with words, dear," Nanny said with a wink.

"It's true I did leave them much sooner than I wanted in my haste to get back to you."

"Leave everything to me, as we discussed earlier. I have a feeling there are answers in Gothel's library that will help you decide what to do about your mothers."

"What do you mean, Nanny?"

"You should ask Snow. I think there is more to this little trip than checking in on Mrs. Tiddlebottom and her sleeping beauties."

CHAPTER VII

MRS. TIDDLEBOTTOM AND
THE MARZIPAN MENAGERIE

Circe perched the odd sisters' house in a field filled with brilliant golden wildflowers at twilight, just as her mothers had done years earlier. Mrs. Tiddlebottom's cottage was silhouetted against a periwinkle sky and surrounded by an overgrown garden with blossoming trees that filled the air with a sticky-sweet scent. Beyond the wildflower field were the cliffs overlooking the ocean.

Snow remembered the scene in Gothel's story in which Gothel snuck out of the cellar to revive herself with the flower before the soldiers came to seize it for their queen. Snow never pictured her as the old witch. She always saw her as young and vibrant with her sisters. And being there in that place where Gothel had felt so alone made Snow's heart ache for all Gothel's hopes and dreams that never had the chance to come true.

Circe and Snow called out to Mrs. Tiddlebottom as they approached the back door, hoping she would pop her sweet face out the kitchen door to say hello, but she didn't respond.

"Mrs. Tiddlebottom?"

The women found Mrs. Tiddlebottom sitting at the kitchen table surrounded by marzipan animals and beautifully decorated birthday cakes. The sweet confections covered the kitchen table and all of the counters, and they were balanced on the window ledges.

"Mrs. Tiddlebottom? It's me, Snow White. I've come with Circe to check on you." The woman said nothing; she just stared off into the distance. "Circe, I think she could use a cup of tea," said Snow, taking the old woman gently by the hand and trying to rouse her.

When Circe went to take the teapot out of the

cabinet, she noticed the candy menagerie had been piled on plates, in bowls, and inside the teacups. She took a marzipan kitten off the top of the teapot and checked inside before preparing the tea.

"Mrs. Tiddlebottom? Do you remember us?" Snow White's heart broke as she looked at the poor woman, who hadn't even noticed them yet. "Mrs. Tiddlebottom?"

The woman finally raised her gaze, and her face lit up when she saw Snow White. "Of course I remember you, dear! I'm so happy you've come back!" Snow White hugged the old woman tightly. "I would offer to make you some tea, but I see sweet Circe is already taking care of things."

Circe blushed. "I'm sorry, Mrs. Tiddlebottom. I thought it would be nice for you to have someone wait on you for a change."

The old woman smiled. "Don't you fret, dear. I am happy you're here."

"I see you've been busy," Snow White said, smiling at the confections scattered around the kitchen.

"Yes, I suppose I have." Mrs. Tiddlebottom

looked around the room as if she didn't know how all the animals had gotten there.

"Maybe we should go into the sitting room or the library while Circe makes us some tea," Snow White said, shooting a concerned look at Circe.

"Oh, I never go into the library. Never! Never the library or the cellar," said the befogged old woman.

"Well, I hope you don't mind my going into Gothel's old library later, Mrs. Tiddlebottom. There are some books in there I think might be of use to us."

Mrs. Tiddlebottom gave Snow a sly look. "Oh, I don't think Gothel would mind. It's not like she can object now, can she?" she said, laughing. "Why don't you just take them? I'd be happy to be rid of the foul things!" She seemed to remember something unpleasant.

"Come on, let's go to the sitting room, Mrs. T." Snow ushered Mrs. Tiddlebottom through the kitchen and dining room, to the lovely little sitting room. The room was cozy and old-fashioned; the walls were covered in brown wallpaper splashed with delicate pink flowers, and the tables with white lace doilies. A perfect home for an old woman. "How are you feeling, Mrs. Tiddlebottom?" The sweet woman looked as if she was considering her answer, but never got around to voicing it. "Mrs. Tiddlebottom?" Snow sat down next to her and took her by the hand. "Mrs. Tiddlebottom, is there anything I can do for you?"

Just then Circe came into the room, carrying a heaping tray. "Ladies, I have the tea. And I've made some little sandwiches."

Mrs. Tiddlebottom looked up at Circe and smiled. "Thank you, dear. I was just about to tell Snow she shouldn't worry about poor old Mrs. Tiddlebottom. I'm fine, dears. Just fine. I have everything I could ever need. Not very many can say that."

Circe put the tea tray down and poured cups for the three of them.

"How are your sleeping beauties?" she asked.

Mrs. Tiddlebottom got a sparkle in her eye and seemed to stir from her waking slumber at the mention of her charges. "Oh, they're just fine. Just fine."

Circe passed Mrs. Tiddlebottom a cup of tea. "Snow was worried you might be a little overwhelmed now that your memories are coming back. We wanted to make sure you are okay."

Mrs. Tiddlebottom put down her tea and reached out for Circe's hand. "Come, sit down with us." Circe sat on the other side of Mrs. Tiddlebottom. "I remember everything. And I'm fine. I promise. I'm just very tired." Snow kissed the old woman on the cheek. "You're such a dear, but really, you girls worry too much." Circe passed Mrs. Tiddlebottom the plate of little sandwiches. "Thank you, dear. May I ask why you're really here? Is it about those books? Oh, don't get me wrong, I know you have kind hearts, the two of you, but this old woman's fairy tale is over. I've done my duty and protected the sleeping beauties, but my job is done, and what I want now more than anything else is to rest."

"What do you mean your job is done?"

"I mean just that, dears. Primrose and Hazel, they woke up a few days ago."

"What? Woke up? But how?" said Circe, getting to her feet. "Where are they?"

"They said they were going home, my dear."

"Home? But how were they brought back to life? How did it happen?"

Mrs. Tiddlebottom smiled. "The flowers, dear. It was the flowers. Didn't you see them when you came in?"

Circe rushed to the window and gasped at the glowing lights coming from the field. "Snow! Look!" The field was filled with brilliant golden flowers. Their light was so bright Circe could see it reflected on Snow White's face. "Mrs. Tiddlebottom, where did these flowers come from?"

Mrs. Tiddlebottom laughed. "Oh, those are Gothel's flowers."

Snow and Circe looked at each other, thunderstruck. "The magic flowers? But how did they get here?"

Mrs. Tiddlebottom laughed again. "Well, dears, they grew, like flowers tend to do."

CHAPTER VIII

SISTERS HAVE SECRETS

It had been many years since Nanny had visited the Fairylands. She never thought she would return after she had helped her sister rebuild it. But now her life had traveled full circle, coming back to this place after Maleficent's death.

She felt the loss of her more profoundly there in the Fairylands, the place where she had raised and loved Maleficent like her own daughter. Remembering the wonderful, smart, and gifted girl she had been. Remembering how her sister had played a part in the destruction of the person she had loved most in the world. But taking a page out of Grimhilde's book, she pushed her feelings deep within her, where they were harder to access. After all, her sister had suffered for her part in Maleficent's death, and she had been admonished by Oberon. Nanny and the Fairy Godmother had forged a tentative bond—one Nanny was afraid of breaking. So she pushed down her feelings. She put them in a place she didn't have to deal with just then. A place where Maleficent lived within her, a secret, private place where the little girl she loved could reside without devouring her from the inside.

She almost longed for the days before she had discovered her true identity—the days when she was just Tulip's nanny, before Pflanze woke her from her long slumber. Things had been so much easier then.

Now, as she looked around the Fairylands, all those feelings she had been struggling to push deep within her bubbled up. For there was her old cottage, and there was Maleficent's tree house, right where she had left it. The sight of it made her cry. She cried over the loss of her adopted daughter, and she cried over giving Aurora to the three good fairies. She cried for all of it. And she cried for herself. But she had to be strong. She had Tulip and Circe to look after now. Though something told her she needn't worry about Tulip any longer. She was becoming the woman Nanny had always known she would be. Circe had set Tulip on that path. She was now smart, adventurous, and independent. She couldn't be prouder of her princess.

Circe was the one who needed Nanny now. Circe was in real danger, because she saw the paths that lay before her. And Nanny thought she knew the road Circe would take. It struck a terrible fear within her heart.

Yes, it was better that Circe was off with Snow White. Better that she wasn't here while the fairies decided her mothers' fate. She didn't think Circe could take hearing one more horrible story about them or some wretched thing they had done in the name of protecting her. She knew the fairies would come to the same conclusions as Circe. The sisters should never be set free. Nanny knew Circe would never be able to thrive in the shadow of her mothers. She would never be able to reach her full potential if she had to keep cleaning up after the maelstrom of her mothers' destructive forces. She would spend the rest of her life making amends for her mothers' foul deeds if they were unleashed on the many kingdoms. The thought was unfathomable.

As Nanny opened her old cottage door, it was like being punched in the chest. The pain of being back there was so alive within her it felt as though this was the place she kept all her secrets, all her pain, all her suffering. It wasn't within her at all; it was here in this cottage. She knew she couldn't stay. Not so close to Maleficent's tree house. Not in the kitchen where she'd fretted over Maleficent's fairy exams. Not in the place she'd spent the most beautiful and painful days of her life.

"Sister, I knew it was a mistake to bring you back here. I can see it on your face." Nanny had almost forgotten her sister was by her side.

"You were right, my dear sister. Can I stay with you after all?"

The Fairy Godmother nodded. "Of course you can."

As she closed the door to her old cottage, and the two fairies made their way to the Fairy Godmother's home, Nanny tried to leave her pain behind. That was where she had been stuffing all her pain, not deep within herself as she had imagined. There wasn't room for much else with Maleficent residing there, so her pain lived in her old cottage, and that was where it would stay until she was ready to revisit it. The farther down the path she got, the less severe her suffering was, until she felt it only in the distant familiar way she had grown to live with. This she could manage. She had lived too many lifetimes, and the memories of those lifetimes were too great to carry around with her. Too heavy. She was happy she had a place to put them.

"Did you say we would be meeting with the other council members today, unofficially, to decide how to proceed?"

The Fairy Godmother gave her sister a sly look.

"I hadn't said so, but I was about to." The ladies laughed.

"Well, I think that is a good idea. Who is on the council now besides you and me?" asked Nanny.

"The three good fairies, the Blue Fairy, and Oberon if he chooses."

Nanny reminded herself that she wanted to send a firefly to Oberon with a message about the meeting in the event her sister had conveniently forgotten. "Do you still employ fireflies to send messages, my sister? I want to send one to Oberon."

The Fairy Godmother wrinkled her nose. "Oberon hears all, my sister, there is no need to summon him. Besides, I am sure he is busy with Tulip, healing the wounded Tree Lords."

Nanny shrugged her sister off. "Well, I want to send him a letter nonetheless, and I'd like to know how Tulip is doing. So if you could direct me to some paper and a quill when we get to your cottage, I would appreciate it."

"Well, here we are now." The two fairies had arrived at the Fairy Godmother's cottage. "Oh! Look at this!" The Fairy Godmother clapped her hands together in delight. "Isn't it lovely?"

The good fairies had apparently been very busy while awaiting their arrival. Fauna, Merryweather, and Flora had decorated the cottage in pink and blue sashes, large glittering bows, and festive banners. The house looked like one of Mrs. Tiddlebottom's birthday cakes, but far more garish. Nanny had forgotten her sister lived in such an idyllic cottage, with its perfect white picket fence and trestles covered in frosting-pink flowers. It was like something out of a fairy tale, and then Nanny laughed. This *was* a fairy tale. They were in the Fairylands, after all.

The three good fairies flitted around the Fairy Godmother like buzzing bees, zooming to and fro and lavishing her with greetings, love, and admiration. And then came a litany of rapid-fire questions that made Nanny's head spin, each of the fairies talking over the others. "So what is this I hear? Have the odd sisters really brought Maleficent back to life?" "Do you think she will be in her dragon form?" "You don't think she can bring back Ursula, do you?" The questions went on unceasingly until Nanny loudly cleared her throat.

"Fairies, fairies, please," the Fairy Godmother said. "I would like to get my sister inside and settled. We can discuss all of this at the council meeting later this afternoon." The three good fairies blushed; they had forgotten to greet Nanny. "Yes, of course, we're so sorry!" said the three fairies. "We will get everything ready for our meeting while you settle in." And they flitted away before Nanny could say hello or good-bye. She laughed, remembering why she hated the Fairylands. How frivolous and silly fairies were, even though she was one herself. It was why she had decided not to wear her wings, and to identify as a witch.

As if she could hear Nanny's thoughts, the Fairy Godmother said, "You realize you will have to wear your wings for the meeting, my sister." Though Nanny's sister didn't share her gift of mind reading, she could often read Nanny's expressions and guess what she might have been thinking.

Nanny frowned. "What about Circe? If she takes your offer, will you fashion her a pair of wings and make her wear them? She is a true witch and has no fairy blood within her, yet you have offered her an honorary wish-granting-fairy position."

Nanny's sister stamped her foot in frustration. "But you *are* a fairy! And you should be proud!"

Nanny didn't want to argue with her. She had to remember her sister had taken on the responsibility of ruling the Fairylands for many years and she really was doing the best job she knew how to do, without Nanny's help or Oberon's. And now Nanny and Oberon were back, telling the Fairy Godmother she'd been doing everything wrong when she had just been doing it the way she'd learned and the way she thought was right. Nanny saw that clearly for the first time and decided she would help her sister make changes in stages; otherwise it would turn the Fairylands upside down. Nanny intended to change everything. She would just have to see what the other fairies had to say. She knew the three good fairies would take the Fairy Godmother's side, but she was almost sure the Blue Fairy would agree with her. And Oberon, well, he always chose what was right.

The more Nanny had thought about it, the more she had come to believe it was the fairies' duty to take care of all those in need—not just the princesses. And that would surely come out at the odd sisters' trial. If Grimhilde and Ursula had had fairies to intervene on their behalf, perhaps the odd sisters wouldn't have destroyed them with their foul, meddling magic.

Nanny knew that wouldn't make sense to someone like the Fairy Godmother—someone sworn by oath to protect the innocent, whether that be a princess in need or a little boy brought to life by the wish of a doll maker. And that meant bringing more fairies into the council, and witches, like Circe, to change the way fairies had been doing their magic for centuries. Their first change would be Nanny taking the Fairy Godmother's place as the head of the Fairylands, but that, too, would have to happen slowly, for fear of hurting her sister.

126

Nanny just had to go about all this as gently as she could.

"Yes, Sister, I will wear my wings if that will make you happy. Should we make our way to meet with the other fairies? Are they waiting for us?"

The Fairy Godmother smiled. "Yes, I hoped we would have time for you to get more settled in, but I do think we should start making our way to Oberon's fountain fairly soon." Nanny took her things to the guest room and sat on the end of the bed for a moment, gathering her thoughts and her courage to make her fairy wings visible. She was in the Fairylands, after all, and perhaps in making these changes, she would finally feel proud to be a fairy.

"Sister! Sister, come quick!" It was the Fairy Godmother. She was screeching from the front room. Nanny ran in.

"What is it?" she asked, looking at the assembled fairies, all crammed into her sister's cottage, and all in a state of panic. "What's happened?"

The three good fairies and the Fairy Godmother

were too upset to speak. It was the Blue Fairy, the ethereal creature of light, who spoke. "Fairy Godmother just got a crow from Oberon. It's the odd sisters. They've somehow managed to escape the land of dreams. They've awoken and left Morningstar."

"But how did this happen? Not even Circe can break the fairy magic keeping them there! How did they escape? Was it Maleficent?"

"Oh dear! I hope not!" the Fairy Godmother said.

"Then who woke them? They didn't wake themselves. Who would be foolish enough to unleash the odd sisters on the many kingdoms?" asked Merryweather.

"I can only think of one creature so loyal to the odd sisters that she would risk everything to set them free," Nanny said. "Pflanze."

CHAPTER IX

LOST FLOWERS

Snow White and Circe sat in Mrs. Tiddlebottom's front parlor, feeling stunned and confused. The flowers had brought Hazel and Primrose back to life, just as Gothel had hoped. Her poor sisters had finally woken up and ventured off to the dead woods.

Alone.

"We have to go there now! They'll be devastated when they see what's happened to the dead woods!" said Snow White, and Circe knew Snow was right.

"Well, my dears," Mrs. Tiddlebottom said, "I will pack you a nice basket if you think you ought to go.

The dead woods aren't too far from here, and I bet that's where they were headed. Back to their home." Mrs. Tiddlebottom went straight to the kitchen and started making them sandwiches for the journey.

"Why in the many kingdoms did she let them leave?" Circe asked, throwing up her hands. She tried not to be frustrated with the old woman, but she couldn't help it.

Snow White frowned at her cousin. "Don't blame her, Circe. She thought she was doing the right thing. They wanted to go home."

"But they have no home to go to! Everything there is ruined. Their sister is dead. They know nothing of the events that happened after their deaths. They're lost and alone, and who knows what kind of powers Primrose has! She has Manea's blood, and they were empowered by all those flowers in the field! And Mrs. Tiddlebottom isn't safe here with all these flowers. You read what Rapunzel's kingdom is capable of doing to possess the flower's magic."

"Circe, calm down. Everything will be fine. Let's pack up Gothel's old library and then go straight to the dead woods. I bet we will get there before Primrose and Hazel do, since they left on foot."

"Okay, that's a good plan," Circe agreed. "Will you ask Mrs. Tiddlebottom if she has some crates so we can pack up the books?"

Snow White smiled. "Of course." And she went off to the kitchen, leaving Circe alone with her thoughts.

Circe. Hello? Are you there?

It was Nanny. Circe took her hand mirror out of her pocket.

Circe! You have to come to the Fairylands as soon as possible. Your mothers escaped from the dreamscape and we are afraid you and Snow are in danger.

"How did they escape?" Circe asked. But she thought she knew.

Circe wiped the mirror without another word, making Nanny's face disappear. "Show me Pflanze!" Circe called out. And then she saw her. The cat lay motionless on the floor of the solarium right where her mothers' bodies had been lying since they had used their magic to destroy Ursula. "Oh, Pflanze!"

Snow ran back into the room, her big eyes wide with worry. "Circe, what's wrong? Is Pflanze here?" She was looking around the room for the majestic creature.

"No, look!" Circe showed Snow the image of the lifeless, beautiful cat in the mirror.

Snow White gasped in horror.

"Pflanze!" Tulip appeared in the mirror, dropping to her knees beside Pflanze. "Oh my goodness, what's happened to you?" Snow and Circe watched her weep over the poor cat.

Snow White touched the mirror, frantically calling out to the princess. "Tulip, is she okay? Is she alive? What happened?"

"The mirror doesn't work that way, Snow. Tulip can't hear us." Circe wiped the mirror again and summoned Nanny. "Show me Nanny."

Nanny's face appeared instantly. *Circe! What happened?*

"I checked in on Pflanze. It looks like something's happened to her. Tulip is with Pflanze now, but I have no way to speak with her."

I'll send word to Oberon. I thought Pflanze had something to do with this. I think it was she who released your mothers from the dreamscape.

"I think so, too. That's why I summoned her. Nanny, if Pflanze used her powers to release my mothers, she may not have survived the ordeal."

I know, my dear. I know. Let me send word to Oberon now so he can check on Pflanze. In the meantime, I want you to take Snow back to her own kingdom, and for you to come directly here to the Fairylands.

"I want to, Nanny, but I can't. We have to go to the dead woods. The rapunzel flower has grown in Mrs. Tiddlebottom's field. Primrose and Hazel have woken up and they're headed there now."

We don't have time for you to be flying off to the dead woods, Circe! Not with your mothers loose! You can't help every single person in need. You'll destroy yourself in the process if you try!

"But, Nanny, we have to! My mothers are responsible for the destruction of Hazel and Primrose's home, and the death of their sister! They've been dead for hundreds of years. I can't just let them stumble upon the ruins of their lives. I can't let them suffer that alone."

Very well, my girl. But please stay safe. Your mothers are going to start searching for you. You have to be quick in the dead woods, my dear. Very quick. Enchant those girls, pack them up, and bring them directly here to the Fairylands if you have to. I want you here with me. I can't lose another daughter. I just can't.

Circe's heart broke for Nanny. "I'll be careful, Nanny, I promise."

I love you, my girl. Now go, and get here as quickly as you can.

"I love you, too, Nanny." And Circe ran her hand across the mirror, making Nanny disappear. She slipped the mirror back into the pocket of her skirt.

"Oh, Snow. If Pflanze released my mothers, I'm afraid we're both in danger. I know how to handle them, but you . . . I'm worried about you."

Snow clenched her jaw, determined. "You're not packing me off to my mother. Listen, Circe. I know you and Nanny are worried about me, but I am older than you, and as much as I appreciate the love and care you have given me, I need you to understand that I am a grown woman and I can make my own decisions. I am going with you to the dead woods. I know I'm not a witch, but I have a feeling more answers are there."

"I believe you. I feel the same way," Circe said quietly. Snow wondered if this was the right moment to tell Circe about her suspicions. Those missing pages she was looking for—what if they were in the dead woods? Perhaps they were with the books Jacob had hidden away from Gothel after her sisters died. Snow didn't know, but she felt as if everything that was happening was leading them to the dead woods.

Circe took something out of her pocket. It was a locket of sorts, a tiny silver flask connected to a chain so it could be worn like a necklace. "Snow, I want you to wear this."

Snow took it into her hand and looked at Circe questioningly. Circe could see that she wanted to ask what was inside but decided against it. The look in her eyes was clear: Snow trusted her cousin.

She didn't need to know what was in the flask. She loved her and wanted nothing more than to go on this adventure with her.

"I'm happy you trust me, Snow. And I hope I'm making the right choice bringing you with me. But promise me you will do whatever I say."

Snow White smiled at Circe, taking her by the hand and squeezing it tightly. "I promise, because I do trust you."

As they hugged, Mrs. Tiddlebottom came into the room. The large hamper in her arms was overflowing with more food than they could possibly need.

"Well, my darlings, please be careful on your journey. Old Mrs. Tiddlebottom isn't a witch, she doesn't pretend to know things the way witches do, but she can smell a fairy tale when it's happening. I'll tell you what I told Primrose and Hazel. My story is at an end, but I feel it's just beginning for you two beauties. Don't let yourselves get caught up in someone else's story. Stick to your own tale, my darlings. Write your own ending if you need to."

Circe gave Mrs. Tiddlebottom a queer look as Snow kissed the old woman on the cheek. "Mrs. Tiddlebottom, there was a mirror in the cellar I asked Snow to bring up for you. If there is anything at all that you need, just call my name and I will appear in the reflection. It's quicker than sending me a message by owl or raven."

Mrs. Tiddlebottom smiled at Circe and Snow. "I don't think I will need it, but I have a feeling you will feel better knowing I will use it if I need to, and you've done so much for me, sweet Circe. This is the least I can do for you. Now go! Let old Mrs. Tiddlebottom rest."

Snow White and Circe packed everything into the odd sisters' house: the hamper of food, the crates of books from Gothel's library, and various trunks. Primrose and Hazel had left everything behind—even their fortune. Circe left Mrs. Tiddlebottom a small chest of coins in her bedroom, enough to keep the woman happy and well fed for many years to come. She didn't think Primrose and Hazel would mind. The woman had cared for them all those years they were dead, after all. It was the least they could do.

After everything was packed and settled, Snow and Circe stood on the front stoop of the odd sisters' house and waved at Mrs. Tiddlebottom, who was standing in the garden. She looked impossibly old to Circe—older, even, than Nanny. "Good-bye, sweet Mrs. Tiddlebottom. Thank you for everything." She looked at her, standing in the sea of magic rapunzel flowers, and wondered if Mrs. Tiddlebottom would ever use them on herself. Wondered if she would choose to live another life. Somehow she doubted it.

"Good-bye, my darlings. Remember what I said: write your own fairy tale, my dears! And take a page out of Mrs. Tiddlebottom's book: stay clear of cellars and bloody chambers!"

Circe and Snow smiled, not knowing quite what to say. They waved good-bye as they went into the house, ready to embark on their own story.

CHAPTER X

THE PLACE
BETWEEN

After being violently ripped from the dreamscape, Lucinda found herself under a large dead tree, its branches twisted and bare, reaching in every direction like grasping hands. The odd sisters knew exactly where they were. This was the place between the world of the living and the world of the dead. The place just before the mists. She and her sisters had been here before.

The place between.

There was one path in the place between, with only two directions: ahead and back. But there was always a choice.

The sisters would choose back. Back to their daughter. Back to their home.

But first they needed to rest. To recover. This was where all those who had lived too long went to rest their bodies and spirits. It was where Nanny had come to rest when she was tired of the world before she went to live with Tulip, and it was where Oberon resided when he took his long slumber. The place between had no mirrors. Lucinda couldn't see what was happening in the worlds beyond. But she could hear if she chose to listen carefully.

She expected to see Maleficent here. They had told her many years earlier to wait for them in this place should she ever die, and they would bring her back to the world. But there was nothing of her here except for her ravens and crows, perched in the massive dead tree, silent specters waiting for their mistress to come back to them. The only one missing was Opal, though they felt as if she had been there. Lucinda knew Maleficent and Opal shared a special bond, forged in childhood and in magic. If anyone could lure Maleficent from beyond the veil, it was Opal. Lucinda looked up at the darkness. The sky resembled a black moth-eaten curtain, scattered with tiny pinholes of light. It didn't frighten her that she couldn't find her sisters Ruby and Martha in this place. They were here, somewhere, just not in her view. She felt them and knew they were well, and that was all that mattered. She needed to rest, and it was better they were each in their own corner of the place between. Thank the gods for Pflanze.

Pflanze's magic was core magic—an unruly magic that resided within and wasn't wielded often, if at all. Creatures with that sort of magic held it in reserve until the time it was needed most, and it usually took them a very long time to build up their reserve again. Lucinda was grateful Pflanze used her magic on this occasion, even if the magic was violent and untamed. Even if it was excruciating being ripped from the dreamscape. They were free, and they were in a place where they could rest and regain their powers. Pflanze had seen to that.

There was so much they needed to do after they left this place, once they were strong and ready to take their position in the world again. She was worried that Maleficent wasn't here as they had discussed, and that Maleficent had found herself too far beyond the veil to come back. That was why they needed Opal. If anyone could lure Maleficent back to the land of the living, it would be her. Lucinda and her sisters would use whatever means were available to raise Maleficent from the dead—even the foul necromantic magic they had learned in the dead woods. They needed their old friend by their side so they could rule in their own lands as they were meant to.

They would take their daughter, Circe, back, and love her as they always had. And if that meant destroying everything and everyone she held dear, then so be it.

For now, though, they would rest. And wait.

Chapter XI

Snow White and the Seven Witches

Circe and Snow White perched the odd sisters' house in the large courtyard below the crumbling mansion in the dead woods. It was as they had imagined. A dead place filled with beauty and steeped in sorrow. A place filled with magic, without its queen to wield it.

They looked out on the city of the dead, just beyond the dense tree line of weeping willows, their branches hanging low and crumbling to dust. The city was still and quiet, but Circe and Snow knew it was likely the dead still resided there.

The Gorgon fountain they had read about in

Gothel's story was still standing with its dancing nymphs frozen in time, as if the Gorgon's enjoyment of their frivolities had inadvertently turned them to stone. Just beyond the courtyard, on the edge of the city of the dead, were Hazel's and Primrose's crypts. Snow and Circe were saddened to see them there, remembering how devastated Gothel had been when she'd lost her sisters. And Circe was sure her mothers had had a hand in their deaths. She just couldn't say how. She thought perhaps she would find the answers in one of her mothers' or Gothel's books.

As she looked out over the woods, Circe was overcome by the destruction her mothers had caused—here and everywhere. There was so much blood on their hands. There had been so much death. And the solution was becoming clearer to her every day. She just didn't have the courage to do it. Not yet.

It was strange for the women to see the place in such ruin, without Sir Jacob or the other minions they'd read about wandering the woods. They almost expected to see them peering out from behind the dead weeping willow trees or resting beneath one of Gothel's weeping angels. They wondered how Primrose and Hazel would feel once they got here. Would they come expecting to see their sister Gothel? It hurt Circe's heart to think they were expecting to find their home just as they'd left it. Yes, this was why it was so important for her and Snow to be here. To tell them their story—and the story of their sister, should they want to know it.

The mansion was in almost complete disrepair, ruined by the soldiers of the kingdom who had come to retrieve the magic flower, forcing Gothel and her sisters from their home many years before. Circe imagined Sir Jacob and his army fighting to protect the dead woods, hoping one day Gothel would return to these lands and take her place as queen of the dead. She felt heartbroken about the ruin of their lives and their home, and of Jacob's hopes and dreams. And to think, all that time, Gothel had been right. The flowers had brought her sisters back to life. If only the flowers Jacob had planted at the little cottage so many years before had bloomed in time.

"Where should we start, Snow? The library? Should we see if it still stands?"

Snow nodded without a word, just as moved as Circe by the state of the dead woods. "Could you maybe repair it?" she asked quietly. "Do you have that power?"

Circe hadn't even thought of that. "I just might. And what a wonderful idea. If Primrose and Hazel intend to live here, then I suppose I'd better try."

"Should we see if . . ." Snow stopped herself.

"What's that, Snow? What did you say?"

Snow squished her lip to the side and bit it, as she often did when she was vexed or unsure about something. "I was going to ask if we should check to see if Sir Jacob survived."

"That's a good idea. Let's check." But Snow was still making that face, causing Circe to think she was unsure.

"Do you think we should disturb him? In Gothel's story, he did say he wanted to rest."

Circe smiled. "You are so kind, Snow. And you're right, he did say that, but I think he would want to know if his witches are about to return."

"How much time do you think we have before Hazel and Primrose get here?"

"Maybe one day more if they're on foot, I think."

"Is that enough time for you to get things in better shape while I take a look in the library and maybe go through the books we took from Mrs. Tiddlebottom's?" Snow desperately hoped she would find the pages from "The Mourning Box."

"Snow, what is this all about, this obsession with missing pages? What is the mourning box?"

"I don't want to say, Circe. Not until I've read the entire story. Please trust me."

Circe took Snow's hand as they walked toward the mansion. "Of course I trust you, Cousin. I trust you with my entire heart. Let's see if the library is still standing, shall we? And then maybe break our fast with something from the feast Mrs. Tiddlebottom packed for us?"

The two ladies made their way up the hill to

what was left of the mansion. Inside, it wasn't as ruined as they had feared. Many of the rooms were still intact and undamaged by the battle. Most of the destruction was to the outer walls and vestibule, and Circe imagined this was what it must have looked like after Manea attacked Gothel and her sisters years earlier. Both of the ladies were happy to see that the morning room they'd read about was still beautiful; only a few panes of glass had been broken, and the furniture hadn't been turned over or damaged like it had in some of the lower rooms.

"This won't take much time at all to manage," said Circe as she and Snow White continued to explore, in search of the library.

The library was one of the older rooms in the mansion, not one of the new rooms Gothel had built for her sisters after she sent her mother's spirit to the mists. It was sad seeing this place, reliving Gothel's story as they walked the paths she must have taken. Snow made herself comfortable in Primrose's old customary seat in the library, the one near the stone carving of a tree that was slightly in bloom. The carving was the one display of life in this dreary place aside from the monstrous stone beasts that were carved into the walls of the older rooms. Snow smiled as she thought of Primrose, and she hoped Primrose was the sweet person she had conjured in her mind after reading Gothel's story.

"I'm going to leave you to your search if you don't mind," Circe said. "I don't have much time to make this place more inhabitable for Hazel and Primrose."

Snow looked up at Circe with her sweet large brown eyes. "And you will look for Sir Jacob?"

Circe smiled and nodded. "Yes, I will look for him." Snow bit her lip. "What's on your mind, Snow?"

"It's just I've been wondering. How were we able to enter the dead woods? Aren't the boundaries enchanted? And even if the minions and Jacob are here, how would you summon them?"

Circe wasn't sure. "I suppose the enchantment died with the last of the witches who ruled here." That didn't seem to satisfy Snow. Circe could tell she had more questions but didn't ask. Circe, too, wondered how her mothers had entered the woods when they were still girls. For now it would remain a mystery. "I have the mirror in my pocket, Snow. Do you have yours?" Snow looked up from the book she had been perusing while they were chatting and nodded. "Call me if you need me. And don't forget to keep that locket on at all times," Circe said.

Snow shook her head and laughed. "I may not be a witch, but I was raised by one. I'll be fine, Circe. Now go. I have a lot of reading to do."

Circe left Snow to her books while she went through the mansion, repairing the damage with the wave of her hand. She expected this sort of magic to be difficult and exhausting, but it was almost effortless. As she swept through the mansion, her magic bringing the house back to its former glory, Circe felt like she was bringing the past back to life, preserving it for Primrose and Hazel, just as Gothel and Jacob had preserved Primrose and Hazel.

Circe found herself back in the courtyard, putting statues in their original positions, and to her surprise she found two striking young women standing before Primrose's and Hazel's crypts, right beneath the words Jacob had etched into stone:

Sisters. Together. Forever.

The women looked exactly as Circe had imagined them.

Primrose had vibrant red hair and a light speckling of freckles across her cheeks and nose. She had soft curves, apple cheeks, and an unmistakable energy about her. Circe could feel Manea's blood running in her veins, though she wondered if the girl sensed it herself. Then there was Hazel. To Circe, Hazel was like an ethereal goddess of the dead. Her long silver hair cascaded over her shoulders and down to her waist. Her face was so pale and luminescent she didn't seem quite human.

Simultaneously, both girls turned to face Circe and smiled. There was no fear or questioning in their eyes. It was as if they knew who she was.

"You must be Circe," said the fiery beauty, Primrose.

Circe flinched. "How do you know who I am?"

Primrose and Hazel looked at each other and

smiled. "We know all about you, Circe. We hoped we would find you here."

Circe walked toward the lovely girls. Seeing the witches home, and alive again, made Gothel's losing them, and their losing her, all the more real. "Then you know about your sister? I'm so sorry."

The girls smiled again. "We know everything, sweet Circe. Please don't worry. Of course our hearts broke for Gothel, but she chose her own path. As you are about to choose yours." Circe wondered how the witches knew so much, but she felt it was rude to ask.

Primrose giggled. "It isn't rude to ask, Circe. We trust you." Circe stood silently, waiting for Primrose to continue. "We've been in the place between since we lost our lives. Gothel tethered us to this world by preserving our bodies, but our spirits resided in another place." Circe was horrified. The idea of Gothel's sisters trapped between this world and the next sent chills through her.

"It was difficult at first—until we learned to listen," said Hazel, who had been, until that moment, silent. Her voice was serene. "I just wish Gothel was with us. I wish she had the same opportunity to listen, and learn. Time to rest, and to recover from what our mother did to us. I wish she'd had the same time we did to let Manea's blood empower her as it has us. Then she would be here, and we could be witches together, as she always wanted."

Circe's heart ached for the three of them, sisters who would never be reunited. She didn't know what to say. Grasping, she said, "You'll be happy to know your beautiful morning room is just as you left it."

Primrose and Hazel looked around. "It seems everything is almost as we left it, thanks to you."

"Shall I walk you up to the house, then? I would like to introduce you to my cousin Snow White. She's in your library, looking for the missing pages to a story that's intrigued her."

Primrose narrowed her eyes. "Missing pages? Are they important?"

"Well, Snow seems to think so. She's been obsessed with reading stories about the dead woods since we read your sister's story."

"Well, if the pages were ripped from the book of fairy tales, I don't think she will find them in our library. Jacob had everything that was important taken from the library and hidden away. He was trying to protect Gothel, to keep her safe from any stories or books that might hurt her or help her to foolishly try to resurrect us without the flower." Circe had to remember these witches probably knew more than she did, having spent so long in the place between. She had to remember they were hundreds of years old. "Yes, though we feel as if we're still your age. And I suppose in body we still are," Primrose said with a smile. "Shall we go find these books and pages that Jacob wisely hid away from my deranged sister?"

Circe hardly knew what to say. It wasn't surprising Primrose would hold that opinion of her sister, but she hadn't expected to hear her say something outright.

"We love our sister, Circe. We do, but we see her clearly. We see her more clearly than she ever saw herself. We had nothing to do in the place between but listen and learn. Don't mistake us, we do mourn her, but we've been mourning her for a very long time, long before she turned to dust and passed into the mists to be with our ancestors."

The three witches walked the paths Circe and Snow had read about, past the weeping angels beneath the dead willow trees, their long hanging branches swaying in the breeze and making the sunlight dance. They reached the crypt Circe remembered from Gothel's story, the one with the large anatomical image of a heart in stained glass. Circe gasped, startling the young witches.

"What is it, Circe? Are you all right?" Circe didn't know how she felt about waking Jacob, if he was there at all. She wasn't sure it was fair, even if they needed his help.

"He will be happy to see you, Circe. Call him."

"Happy to see me? He doesn't even know me." Circe felt as if the witches knew far more than they were sharing.

"He knows of you. Your mothers spoke of nothing else. Wrote of nothing else in their missives."

Primrose and Hazel were smiling at Circe like she was an old friend, not like she was someone they had just met. It was strange, this feeling of familiarity they seemed to have with her, and how comfortable she felt with them. How oddly at home she was in this strange and beautiful place.

"But that wasn't me. That was their real sister. That Circe, the one they wrote of, she died," Circe said in a small voice.

"Oh, you are her, Circe. You are real, and you were always meant to be. Now, please call Sir Jacob. I promise he will answer if he is within," said Hazel, urging Circe to be brave.

"What are the words?" Circe felt she was on the edge of something. She felt that in doing this, she would somehow be changing her life forever.

"You're right, wise witch," Hazel said, reading Circe's thoughts. "Now use your own words and summon Jacob."

Circe took a deep breath, and she said the words. Words that came not from a spell book, but from her heart.

"Sir Jacob, the living are in need of you once more. If anyone is deserving of rest, it is you. So, please, forgive our intrusion and know it pains me to rouse you from your slumber." Primrose and Hazel smiled as they heard Circe's choice of words. Circe could see they approved.

The door to the crypt opened slowly, with the terrible sound of stone moving against stone. Circe understood now why it had set Gothel's teeth on edge when she heard it.

Jacob stood in the open doorway, squinting against the sunlight. He looked much the way Circe had expected. Exceedingly tall and large boned, and she could tell he had once been very handsome. He held his top hat to shield his eyes from the sun as he slowly made his way out the crypt door. As his eyes adjusted, he saw them. He saw his witches. His Primrose and Hazel. His face twisted into his customary strained smile, and it sent joy into Circe's heart to see it. Both girls rushed to their dear old friend, hugging him around the waist. Then he looked up and saw Circe. She saw it wash over him:

a look of recognition she hadn't expected. If she hadn't known better, she would have thought the man knew her. Loved her. And was happy to see her.

"Well, the one made from three has finally come to the dead woods. But does she bring her mothers crashing down on us, as it was foretold, or have they been safely stowed away, as the ancestors hoped?"

Circe was taken aback, too confused even to answer.

Sir Jacob looked to Primrose and Hazel. "She doesn't know, then?"

The witches shook their heads. "No," Primrose said. "She came here with Snow White seeking answers about her mothers. I think it's time she learned the truth."

Chapter XII

Always Lucinda

Snow White was sitting in the morning room with a stack of books she had brought up from the library. She liked this room better than the others. What little light there was in the dead woods filtered through the windows, giving the room an almost cheerful glow. She felt sad that Gothel had never been able to truly appreciate the room the way she'd wanted to with her sisters. Snow couldn't help remembering reading about the solstice party Gothel had thrown for her sisters, and about how much she'd wanted them to love living in this house together.

A voice interrupted her musings. "Snow, we have company."

Snow looked up and saw Circe standing in the doorway with two beautiful young women. All three of them were holding stacks of papers and books.

"Primrose! Hazel!" Snow White stood up from her little window reading nook and rushed to the young witches, embracing them as if she had known them for many years and was not meeting them now for the first time.

Primrose smiled. "I knew you would be sweet," she said as the witches put down the books and papers. "And so pretty. I hadn't expected you to be quite so pretty." Snow White blushed deeply, lowering her eyes. She was never comfortable with people commenting on her beauty. It wasn't something that was important to Snow. It wasn't where she got her self-worth. Watching her mother's obsession with vanity, she had learned at a young age that a woman's true virtue resided in her heart.

"Here, come sit down. I just made a pot of tea

and there is plenty for all of us. I'll just go get us some more cups."

Hazel took Snow's hand. "No, dear. I will have Jacob arrange for that."

Snow looked around for the man she had read about. "Jacob? But where is he?"

Hazel looked toward the entryway. "He's just out there. He was afraid his appearance would frighten you."

Snow rushed to the entryway and found Jacob right around the corner. "Jacob, I am so happy to meet you." She put her hands on the sides of his face. "You are just as beautiful as I imagined. It's no wonder Manea was so in love with you." Jacob didn't say anything as Snow White led him into the morning room to sit with her and the witches. "Everyone, please sit down and have some tea." Primrose laughed, and suddenly Snow felt foolish for acting as the hostess in the witches' home. "I'm sorry, of course it's your place to offer the tea. I didn't mean—"

Hazel stopped Snow before she could continue. "No, Snow, you're fine. We always imagined you would be a sweet woman, and we're just pleased to see you in real life." Snow White felt the same way. She was in awe of these witches, brought to life from the pages of Gothel's story. To have just read about Hazel and Primrose, thinking she would never have the opportunity to meet them, and to be in their home speaking to them was the most magnificent thing she'd experienced in many years.

Jacob cleared his throat, drawing her attention. "I understand you were looking for some missing pages. May I inquire which story you were reading? I might be able to help."

Snow White bit her lip, afraid to answer Jacob. She couldn't bear to admit the story was about him. It didn't seem proper to ask him to provide the story of his death. She didn't want to hurt him. "Don't be afraid, Snow. Jacob is here to help us. We could never imagine you hurting anyone on purpose," Primrose said.

Snow White smiled and asked playfully, "So you can read my mind as well? Am I surrounded by mind readers, then?"

Primrose laughed. "We cannot read your mind, sweet Snow, but we can read Circe's. And she can read yours. So I guess in a way we know what you were thinking. It's all very strange, isn't it? And it must be maddening. We'll do our best not to drive you to distraction with it. I remember dreading others knowing how I was feeling or what I was thinking, and now I find it quite comforting."

"I suppose it does make things easier," Snow said with a laugh, then turned her attention back to Jacob. "Dear Jacob, I was reading a story involving you and Manea in the book of fairy tales. Her mother was threatening to kill you. The title of the story was 'The Mourning Box.'"

Jacob became unsteady on his feet, losing his balance and almost falling. "Jacob! Please sit down." Snow White rushed to help him to a seat and got him a cup of tea. "Here, dear man, drink this." Snow White looked down at him as she handed him his tea. His eyes were beautiful, or at least she thought they might have been once upon a time when he was alive. She could almost see the man he once was, and her heart broke as she remembered the story "The Mourning Box." Primrose and Hazel rushed to Jacob and sat on either side of him, each taking one of his hands. Snow could see Jacob wasn't used to this sort of attention and it made him uncomfortable, but she could also see he was so happy to have the young witches back that he wasn't about to protest.

Snow White laughed quietly to herself. The poor man was besieged by witches. Circe kneeled down in front of him and put her hand on his knee.

"Jacob, are you quite all right? Is there something I can do for you? I'm so sorry if our coming here has upset you."

"No, my little witch. You are more than welcome here. I have been expecting you for a very long time. Your coming was foretold by the ancestors." Circe's face was full of confusion. "I think you'd better read this." Jacob handed Circe the stack of papers he had been holding. It looked like they had been torn out of a book.

"'The Mourning Box'! This is the story Snow was reading?"

Snow took the pages from Circe, her heart racing. "It is." She went to her stack of books, took the fairy tale book from the pile, and handed it to Circe. "I really should have told you about this before now, but I wanted to be sure I wasn't jumping to wild conclusions before I did."

"Your conclusions are far from wild," said Primrose, smiling at Snow White.

"Here, I think you should all read this first," Snow said, showing them the book of fairy tales, which was open to "The Mourning Box."

"Oh, we already know the story," said Primrose. "And I daresay Jacob couldn't forget it if he tried."

Snow White blushed and handed the book to Circe, who immediately became engrossed in the story. "Of course he couldn't. My heart has been filled with dread ever since I read it. But I wonder, who tore those pages out?"

"I did, sweet majesty," Jacob said. "I was trying to protect my poor little witch, Gothel. I promised her mother I would keep her secrets. And now, well, it seems I may have caused more harm by keeping them."

"You did right to try to protect her, Jacob. Truly. Please don't blame yourself." Snow held back a tear. "I always thought the fairy tale book belonged to the odd sisters. How did you come to have it?"

Jacob's face contorted into a strange smile. "And so it does. But it wasn't always so." Snow thought she understood what he meant. Everything had been leading her and Circe here, to the dead woods. Everything she had suspected since she read Gothel's story was now playing out.

Circe gasped. She looked as if some invisible creature had stolen the life from her. She looked like a ghost, her eyes wide with terror.

"Circe, what's wrong?" asked Snow. "Did you read the story?" Circe nodded, unable to speak, taking everything in.

Snow went to her side, putting her arm around her cousin. "Shall we read the rest together, then, dear cousin? Don't be afraid. I will be right here."

✣ ✣ ✣

*M*anea *was crumpled in a heap over Jacob's dead body.*
Her mother had slashed his throat. Manea was weeping so
hard she couldn't catch her breath.

She had made her choice and lost her dearest love.

"Mother . . . please . . . don't take . . . my baby!"
She could hardly get the words out. She felt like she was
choking on them along with her overwhelming grief. She
felt as if she were trapped in a nightmare from which she
couldn't wake. All she could do was weep. She was help-
less. Her mother was too powerful and would do anything
she wanted with her daughter. Manea looked up at Nestis
with pleading eyes. "Mother, please."

Nestis put her hand on her daughter's head, patting
her like a broken and neglected child or a beloved pet.
"My darling girl, please stop crying. I promise you will be
happy with your daughters."

Manea felt the ruin of her life crashing down on
her. She had betrayed her dearest love to try to save her
daughter, and her mother was going to do with her what
she willed anyway. Manea didn't dare try to use what

little powers she possessed against her mother. She knew she wasn't strong enough. Her mother could kill with a single look if she desired.

"My sweet, confused daughter, this was your choice. You could have had Jacob and your daughters, but you chose to stand against me and suffered the consequences."

Manea cried even harder, sobbing into Jacob's chest. "My dearest love, I am so sorry. I'm so sorry. Please forgive me. Oh, please forgive me."

Nestis lost her patience with Manea and sent her crashing violently across the room with a wave of her hand. "Stop this nonsense at once, Manea! I won't have a daughter of mine degrading herself over a human!" She cradled the baby girl in her arms. "Now compose yourself at once, and start conducting yourself as the future queen of these lands! Do you understand?" She didn't wait for Manea's reply. She turned and exited the room with the child, leaving Manea alone.

With Jacob's body.

Manea's hands and dress were covered in his blood from her trying to stop the bleeding. She sat there crying over the loss of him, and over the loss of the relationship she'd thought she had with her mother.

And over the loss of her daughter. Her darling girl.

What would she do?

She didn't know how to contact the ancestors without the mourning box. Her mother had destroyed it.

They had promised all would be well. They had promised they wouldn't let it go too far.

She had to trust them. Trust they wouldn't let anything happen to her daughter.

As she sat there, wondering what was to come, her mother's skeletal minions came into the room, their bones rattling and scraping along the stone floor. She had grown up with these silent, morose creatures skulking about the house. Her mother used them like servants. They were always about, ready to do her mother's bidding. Manea couldn't stand the sight of them. When she was queen of these lands, she would have them shut away so she wouldn't have to feel their empty, hollow eye sockets always watching her. Without ceremony, the skeletal grotesqueries gathered up Jacob's body. "Where are you taking him?"

Manea cried. But they didn't answer. They never did. She couldn't stand their silence. It was worse than the cacophony of a thousand harpies and, to Manea, more deadly. She felt like she could drown in the absence of their words.

Manea sat huddled in the corner, covered in her lover's blood, as she watched the skeletal minions take him away.

She looked at the empty crow's nest cradle, where her daughter should have been, and felt numb. She had no choice other than to wait and see what happened. Her mother was too strong. She was queen of these lands. And the ancestors would do nothing beyond making sure her mother didn't try to extend her reach past the forest of the dead. She had never felt so alone, so afraid, and so filled with dread.

Outside, the sky was turning lilac. It seemed like another world outside the nursery windows, and she was afraid to face it. Afraid to live in a world without Jacob. Afraid to live in a world with a mother who would do this to her. So she sat alone, waiting for her mother to return. Waiting for her to bring her daughter back to her. Her daughters, she reminded herself. Soon she would have three. Would she be able to tell her own daughter from the abominations her mother was creating? Would she know which one she had brought into the world herself and which were created by magic?

"They are all your daughters, my darling girl. Each of them. And I know you will love them all equally."

Nestis stood in the doorway between two of her skeletal minions. Each of them was holding a baby. Manea's head spun and the room swayed; everything was going in and out of focus as she desperately tried to pick her own daughter out of the three before her.

"Behold your daughters, Manea." Her mother was beaming as she and the minions put the babies into the crow's nest cradle. "Look at them, my love. They're perfect."

Manea got up slowly. She felt as if she were treading water. This must be a nightmare. It couldn't really be happening. But there they were, all three of them, perfect, beautiful, and unharmed.

"They will be the most powerful witches this land has ever seen! Mark my words, Manea. Your daughters will be the ruin of all our enemies!"

"What have you done? What will my daughters become?"

Nestis laughed in a way Manea had never heard her mother laugh before; it sounded wicked and cruel, and full of madness and contempt. "They will bring darkness to the world, my sweet. Their murder ballads will be heard in every kingdom!"

Manea looked at her daughters and couldn't tell one from the others. The three were identical, mirror images of each other. "Which one is mine?" she asked, but her mother just laughed harder.

"They are all your daughters, Manea."

"But which of them is Lucinda?" she screamed, making all the babies but one cry. And then she knew. Something within her told her this one was Lucinda. Her true daughter. The first.

"They are all Lucinda. They will always be Lucinda. They are one," said Manea's mother. "But give them their own names. Give them their own power. Give them your love and guidance. They are yours. All of them."

Nestis left Manea alone in the nursery with her daughters. Manea picked up Lucinda, looking down on the other two.

"Ruby," she christened one. "And Martha," she said, looking down on the innocent babies in their nest. "Lucinda, Ruby, and Martha.

"But always, always Lucinda."

CHAPTER XIII

MURDER IN THE
DEAD WOODS

The crows circled the dead woods, obscuring the sunlight like ominous, lurid clouds. Their caws and screeches were otherworldly, and terrifying.

Snow White and the witches put down the pages from the fairy tale book and ran to the large morning room windows, pressing themselves against them, watching the creatures circling closer and closer. Snow gasped. "Who sent them?"

Circe didn't know. They seemed somehow familiar to her, but she could feel nothing from them. It was the strangest thing, feeling nothing from these creatures. There was no life force within them. None at all.

"They are not alive, Circe. They're dead things, sent by your mothers."

Circe's heart skipped a beat. "Hazel, are you sure? I didn't know my mothers employed crows or could command the dead!"

Primrose squinted at the striking birds, as if she was trying to take their measure, to feel something perhaps Circe was unable to detect. "They're Maleficent's birds, but they were sent by the odd sisters."

Something about that terrified Circe. "Are my mothers dead, then? Or have they sent Maleficent here to destroy us?"

"No, they are not dead, but they command the dead—like their mother and her mother before them. And they are coming here to take what they think is their rightful place among them," said Hazel.

"What does she mean, Circe? Your mothers are coming here?" Snow White panicked.

Circe didn't understand how the witches knew so much, but she trusted them. She didn't know why, but she did. "I have to get Snow out of here," she said, looking at the witches. "I'm sorry. But my mothers have a vendetta against Snow White, and she's in danger if she stays here. We have to go!" Circe had taken Snow by the hand and was ready to flee. She hated the idea of leaving Jacob, Primrose, and Hazel to contend with the odd sisters alone, but she felt she had made a mistake in bringing Snow White here, and she wanted to get her out of the dead woods at once. "I will come back. I promise I won't leave you here alone for too long. I just want to get Snow safely away," said Circe, feeling conflicted. And feeling trapped.

"Your mothers move among the ravens, they float upon the breeze, they move among shadows, they walk across the sea, they move among the candles, they float among the smoke, and they move something deep inside of me," said Hazel, her gray eyes somber.

"What are you saying, Hazel?" asked Circe, still

panicking at the thought of her mothers swooping down on Snow White.

"My sister is saying your mothers are everywhere. You can't escape them, so you might as well face them here," Primrose said. Her wide, friendly smile hadn't wavered, not once since they had arrived.

"But what of Snow?"

"This is Snow's story, too, dear Circe. All our fates are connected. Haven't you guessed this yet?" asked Hazel.

"Snow White is not a witch!"

"True, but her mother is, and though they may not be related by blood, there is a bond between them so pure and so deep she has become entangled in this fairy tale nevertheless."

"How soon before they get here?" asked Circe, looking out the window and watching the crows.

"We still have time. Your mothers are not strong enough to make their way here, not yet," said Hazel, contemplating the crows along with Circe as if she got her information from them.

"Yes, we have time. More time than we need,

really. There's still so much you don't know. And we want you with us when you learn the truth. We want to help," said Primrose.

Circe had thought she was coming here to help Primrose and Hazel. She thought they would be alone, frightened, and lost. But it turned out *she* was the one who was lost. It was she who needed help. And she was thankful the witches were here with her. Thankful to be home.

This is my home. Circe felt for the first time as if she was in a place she truly belonged. She felt at home at Morningstar, and in her mothers' house, of course, but this place was different. She felt like she truly belonged in the dead woods. She felt a connection to it, by blood and by right. This was where she would stay. This was the place she would call home. It comforted and frightened her at once.

"That's right, my dear. You are home. This is your land as much as it is ours. You were born of Lucinda, Ruby, and Martha. You will inherit the dead woods after your mothers pass," said Hazel.

This was all too much. Circe was angrier with

her mothers than she had ever been before. There was so much they had been keeping from her. So many secrets.

"Why didn't they grow up here? Why didn't my mothers tell you who they were when they first came here so many years ago, when you were all girls together?"

Jacob, who had been sitting quietly in his chair, finally spoke. The sudden sound of his deep voice startled the witches and Snow, who had forgotten he was there. "Manea sent our daughters away. But you're right, Circe, my granddaughter. There is much more to the story."

Circe hadn't even put that together. She was too worried about Snow and her mothers. She felt muddled, confused, and overwhelmed. Jacob was her grandfather.

"Of course you're muddled and confused, sweet Circe. Jacob understands," said Primrose, reading Circe's mind. "This is too much for even the strongest of witches. And you are the strongest witch of the age. Even stronger than your mothers. Stronger than our mother, and her mother before her. You have the power to stop your mothers, Circe. We just hope you choose the right way."

Jacob got up from his seat and put his hand on Circe's cheek. "Oh, how I wish Manea had your strength and power. None of this might have happened. I wish I had never allowed our daughters to be sent away only to come back and destroy everything."

Primrose took Jacob's hands tenderly in hers. "Lucinda, Ruby, and Martha were meant to take this path no matter. This isn't your fault, Jacob," she said.

"How do you know all of this? It's uncanny. Witches or not, you know so much," said Circe, looking at Primrose and wondering how it was possible they could all know so much about her and her mothers.

"Everything can be heard in the place between if you listen hard enough," Primrose said. "We had nothing else to do but listen. As your mothers were always behind the mirrors, watching, we were always behind the veil, listening."

The idea sent chills through Circe. And she suddenly felt afraid her mothers were listening to them now. "Do you think my mothers are in the place between? Do you think they are listening?"

"I do," said Hazel. "I feel them, but they are still very far away."

CHAPTER XIV

THE FAIRY COUNCIL

Nanny watched the Fairy Godmother flit about, getting everything ready for the fairy council meeting. She was putting out the tea and little cakes and arranging cookies decorated with pink frosting. And she was setting out her best preserves for the biscuits. If Nanny hadn't known better, she'd have said her sister was preparing for a tea party and not making a battle plan to stop the odd sisters from trying to destroy the Fairylands.

"Sister, can you get the pink rose-pattern tea set? I have so much to do, and I could use some help," said the Fairy Godmother as she set a plate of cherry tarts on the table. Nanny conjured the set with a wave of her hand. "I wish you would use your wand!" said the Fairy Godmother, giving her sister a nasty look, or at least the closest thing to a nasty look the Fairy Godmother could manage. If anyone else had seen the look on her face, they wouldn't have guessed she was cross with Nanny. "It's what a real fairy would do."

"Why should I use a wand when I don't need to?" Nanny was trying not to be annoyed with her sister, but since they'd been back to the Fairylands, her sister was becoming more fairylike by the day.

"And don't forget to make your wings visible!" the Fairy Godmother squealed.

Nanny sighed. "Yes, Sister."

"Don't roll your eyes at me, Sister! Did you know there are humans who have wished with all of their hearts they had fairy wings? And here you are, dreading wearing them!" said the Fairy Godmother, tutting at her sister.

"I'd happily give them to someone who wants them more than I do. You know that. Now let's please change the subject before we become even more cross with each other," said Nanny.

The Fairy Godmother conjured lovely plates, doilies, and a beautiful four-layer pink-and-blue cake. "Yes, of course you're right! Have you spoken to Tulip? Did she mention if Oberon would be attending the meeting?"

"She didn't say. They've both been occupied with their adventures."

"I don't know about that young lady! Romping about with the likes of the Tree Lords. What will her parents think?"

"I fear this is another topic we won't agree upon, dear sister."

"Fine! Maybe we should just focus on getting ready for the meeting. Just pop some bows on the backs of these chairs, then, won't you? The other fairies will be here any moment!"

"Bows?" Nanny was aghast.

"Goodness, you're no help! I'll take care of it myself, then!" The Fairy Godmother waved her wand with an air of annoyance as she conjured gaudy pink bows on the backs of the seats around the council table. She stood back and surveyed her work. "It looks lovely, don't you think?"

Nanny looked around, laughing to herself as she realized, what with the blooming cherry blossoms and the Fairy Godmother's decorations, she was surrounded by the color pink. She was in the Fairylands. She asked the gods to give her the strength to be patient with the fairies. Especially her sister.

As Nanny and the Fairy Godmother finished up their preparations, the other fairies on the council began to assemble. Nanny and her sister had set everything up in the courtyard, near a fountain with a life-sized statue of Oberon at the center. Cherry blossoms had fallen into the water and were littering the cobblestones. Being there again, Nanny started to feel the pangs of heartbreak as she remembered Maleficent. But she pushed them away. She hated that Circe was so far away, especially now that her mothers were at large and Grimhilde was up to something. And what if the odd sisters could truly summon Maleficent from the dead? How would

Nanny be able to face her? She tried to push all her fears away. At least she wasn't afraid for Tulip. She was safe with Oberon. He would protect her. One less person to worry about.

But Circe. Nanny hadn't heard from her, and she was starting to fret. "Sister, I'm going to slip away and talk to Circe, just for a moment. I'm worried about her."

"There isn't time. Everyone is here."

Nanny sighed.

"And I see you've forgotten your wings!" the Fairy Godmother added, tapping her sister on the back with her wand. "Bibbidi-bobbidi-boo! There you go!" Nanny took a deep breath, willing herself not to be angry with her sister. She hated that bibbidi-bobbidi nonsense. And she hated her wings.

Nanny could never stand the weight of them. They felt oppressive and heavy. She remembered talking to Maleficent when her charge was still rather small, lamenting her lack of wings. *My darling, wings are not all they're cracked up to be! I promise, you are not missing a thing.* Nanny had to laugh. How did she find herself here in the Fairylands, doing her sister's bidding and wearing wings? *You think fairies have freedom because they can fly wherever they want, my little fairy-witch?* she had once said to Maleficent. *Well, my dear, you have more freedom without them. One day you will understand. You will be happy you don't have wings.*

All the fairies were assembled in the courtyard, cooing over the decorations and gossiping about the news of the odd sisters. "Fairies, fairies, please take your seats!" said the Fairy Godmother, clapping her hands like a stern headmistress trying to get the fairies' attention, then taking the center seat with her back to the cherry blossom tree. "Sister, sit here to my right." She tapped the chair next to her several times with her wand, sending up a spray of glittering sparks with each tap. Nanny didn't think she meant to sound bossy, but there was always something in her sister's demeanor that made her come off that way. The same went for Merryweather, her sister's favorite, who was taking delight in scolding Fauna and Flora.

"Fauna! Flora! Sit down," the fairy barked. "Look at this splendid feast that has been laid out for us! And on such a beautiful day! Now be careful not to splash any tea or spill the jam on the lovely table-cloth."

Nanny laughed. "It's always a beautiful day in the Fairylands, is it not? I can't imagine it ever being gloomy here. My sister wouldn't have it!"

The three good fairies laughed nervously. Only the Blue Fairy looked at ease in Nanny's company. "Hello, Nanny. I'm so pleased to see you again." Nanny never quite got used to the Blue Fairy's luminescence, but she always found her to be such a lovely soul, the very embodiment of what Nanny thought a fairy should be. Kind, loving, and nurturing.

"I'm so happy to see you!" said Nanny. She wanted to tell her that she'd always held a place for her in her heart, ever since the Blue Fairy had supported Maleficent during the fairy exams many years earlier. But she didn't want to make the other fairies uncomfortable. So she just smiled at the Blue Fairy, hoping she knew the esteem she felt for her.

"Now, once we all have our teacups and plates full, I'd like to start the meeting! We are here to discuss the very serious matter of the odd sisters," said the Fairy Godmother, piling little pink cakes on her rose-patterned plate. "Oh, Merryweather! I think you will like these little cakes we have today! They're lemon poppy seed, your favorite! And, Fauna, you will simply swoon when you taste the rose hips tea! The honey Flora gave me from her garden is delicious. Everyone must try it!" The Fairy Godmother's chirping about the various delights on the table was driving Nanny to utter distraction. "Oh! It looks like we're already running out of little cakes! Well, there we go!" she said, filling the three-tiered cake stand once again with a gleeful smile.

Nanny couldn't help feeling her sister wasn't taking the situation seriously at all. This was exactly the sort of thing that frustrated Nanny about the Fairylands: the needless frivolity in the face of destruction. Earlier that day her sister had been sputtering and in a panic, and now she was making tea and serving cakes rather than calling a war council as she should. Was there something in the water in the Fairylands that made everyone giddy and dim-witted? Nanny cleared her throat, making the Fairy Godmother give her the side-eye. "I'm sure my sister, the One of Legends, though here we affectionately call her Nanny, would like us to get down to business. She has been long away from the Fairylands and forgets her fairy ways," said the Fairy Godmother, giving Nanny a look that didn't deter her from taking a more serious approach than her sister was taking.

"The odd sister situation *is* quite serious, and I think we do need to get down to business before we are faced with the destruction of the Fairylands once again," said Nanny. She continued before her sister could answer. "We should be sending for Oberon and his Tree Lords and anyone else willing to fight at our side to defend us, not drinking tea and conjuring bows!"

"Now listen, I know you ruled the Fairylands

after Oberon left, but you abandoned your post and left it to me. I won't have you barking orders at my own table!"

The Blue Fairy smiled at the Fairy Godmother. "I'm sorry, Godmother, but I think Nanny may have a point. If Oberon hadn't learned of the odd sisters' plan to rouse Maleficent's spirit from the dead, we would never have known. Quite honestly, I'm surprised he isn't already here, making plans to defend the Fairylands. And now we find that the odd sisters have been released from the dreamscape. I'm sorry, Godmother, but Nanny is right. Something has to be done at once!"

"The odd sisters have always been a menace. From the moment I saw them, I knew they would be nothing but ruin and chaos!" said the Fairy Godmother.

"Oh, poppycock!" spat Nanny, getting frustrated with her sister. "They were babies when you first laid eyes on them! How could you possibly have seen?" Nanny looked at the fairies' shocked faces. Clearly they had never seen anyone stand up to the

Fairy Godmother, who looked like a perturbed bird shaking water off her feathers, she was so angry.

"Now listen here! The odd sisters' offenses will be heard! They will go down in the records!" she said, shaking.

"They *are* in the records! In the book of fairy tales! One only has to read it to see their various offenses!" said Nanny, upset that her sister was wasting time.

"I will have them down in fairy record!" screeched the Fairy Godmother. "Their evildoing has been going on for far too long! Allow me to present my case against them." She cleared her throat. "Charge number one: Snow White. The odd sisters tormented the poor girl and drove her mother mad, encouraging her to murder Snow! Thank goodness she only succeeded in putting her in an enchanted sleep! And they gave Snow White a mirror with the ghost of Grimhilde trapped within! And if that's not enough, they are *still* invading the girl's dreams after all these years. Charge number two: Belle. The sisters encouraged Circe to curse the poor Beast, the misunderstood creature that he was, and his entire household. But Belle was the real victim here. They cast devious spells to send poor Belle into the woods to be devoured by wolves!" The Fairy Godmother cleared her throat again. "Charge number three: Ariel. As if the previous charge wasn't reprehensible enough, they plotted with Ursula to kill Ariel! Not to mention their plans to take Triton off the throne, and they almost succeeded in killing Prince Eric. Let the record reflect there are two additional victims for this charge! Charge number four: Aurora. They helped Maleficent by means of foul, putrid dark magic to create Aurora! And though we love our princess, my goodness, that poor girl, what if she actually did take after her mother? That was completely irresponsible of them to put a future princess in danger like that! Charge number five: Rapunzel! They colluded with and helped that horrid baby-snatching witch Gothel to conceal Rapunzel's whereabouts from her heartbroken and worried family!"

Nanny rolled her eyes. Yes, everything her sister

had just said was true. But it wasn't the entire story. As usual, she didn't take the victims who were not princes or princesses into account.

"Yes, let the record reflect the various charges we intend to bring against the odd sisters during their trial, should we actually survive their attack," said Nanny, casting a serious look at her sister. "I know some of you are going to have a hard time with this, but I do feel it's partially our fault the odd sisters have gone so far. If Maleficent had someone looking after her, the odd sisters wouldn't have taken it upon themselves to try to help her by creating a daughter for her."

"Nanny," said the Blue Fairy gently, "you know I've always had a fondness for Maleficent, but I have to say, she did have a fairy looking out for her: you."

Nanny looked into the Blue Fairy's eyes, and she saw only sweetness and none of the malice the other fairies had when they spoke of Maleficent.

"Yes, but I failed her. If I had stood by her and protected her, searched harder for her, none of this would have happened. Maleficent would never have become an unfeeling monster if she hadn't given all the best parts of herself to her daughter. She would still be with us today. I failed her. The fairies failed her, and we need to take responsibility by making sure this never happens to another young woman or young man in need again." Nanny took measure of the fairies and saw only the Blue Fairy seemed to agree with what she was saying. She continued, hoping with all her heart she would be able to bring them around to her way of thinking.

"I feel we need to revisit the idea of who the fairies help. Maleficent had a very good case for this when she sat for her fairy exams. She felt it was Grimhilde who needed help in Snow White's scenario, and I have to agree. Maleficent overheard the man in the mirror tormenting Grimhilde, and decided to help her, and was penalized for not helping Snow White when it was clear it was Grimhilde who was in danger!"

"Grimhilde in danger? Are you serious? She tried to kill her own daughter!" spat the Fairy Godmother. The three good fairies chimed in with murmurs of agreement. Each of them talked over the others, their voices becoming shrill in defense of the Fairy Godmother.

"If Grimhilde had had a fairy to help her through her grief, not to mention someone to protect her from her abusive father, she would never have turned to the odd sisters, gone mad, and tried to kill her daughter. Maleficent saw this! Maleficent saw that by trying to help Grimhilde, she was also helping the princess Snow White!"

"Maleficent sided with Grimhilde because they are both evil!" hissed the Fairy Godmother.

"Oh! I would have guessed that would still be your stance on this, Sister! Perhaps if you could have gotten past your fairy bias, you would have seen the special, talented girl Maleficent was before we failed her. Before you sent her on her path of ruin."

The Fairy Godmother got up from her seat and slammed her fists on the table, rattling the teapot and making the teacups quiver. "Now hear, Sister! We are not going to dredge all of this up again! I won't stand accused of Maleficent's death once more!

And what does this have to do with the odd sisters? Can you tell me that?"

"It has everything to do with them. It's for all women like them who are not born beautiful princesses and therefore must live without the guidance and support of the fairies! How would the odd sisters have turned out if they had had a proper fairy to look after them? Look at Gothel, and Ursula. Had they had fairies looking after them, their lives may have turned out so much differently!"

"They're witches!"

"Circe is a witch! And yet you want to make her an honorary wish-granting fairy! Do you choose her because of her beauty or because she is a gifted, empathetic witch?"

"I choose her because of the good she has done with Tulip, and with Belle. I choose her because she is a gifted young witch, and I wanted to steer her away from her mothers, if you want to know the entire truth! Of course it doesn't hurt that she is beautiful. She won't frighten her charges like Maleficent did during her exams." This made the three good fairies giggle, causing Nanny to give them a wrathful look.

"It's not Maleficent's fault you couldn't see past her horns and her green skin!"

"No, my sister, I couldn't see past her black heart! Just as I couldn't see past Gothel's and Grimhilde's black hearts!"

Nanny shook her head. "If these wretched fairies hadn't stolen Maleficent's birds, and if you hadn't said those dreadful things the day of the fairy exams, she would never have exploded into a rage of fire and destruction! I should never have given you her daughter, never have let you fools give her to King Stephan and his queen! Oh, I know they longed for a child, and I know they met the fairy criteria for being good, loving parents, and why not turn the girl into a princess! But in doing so, I betrayed my foster daughter and broke her heart, and that is why she turned to Lucinda, Ruby, and Martha for help!"

"You fail to remember why the fairies don't take witches on as charges, dear sister. Look to your first charges as example."

"How dare you bring that up!"

"Every witch you have ever tried to help has broken your heart and caused more destruction and death. Why do you think we tried to bring Circe into our ranks, if not only to save her from you, and her mothers?"

Nanny felt as though her sister had struck her in the face. "The odd sisters were babies then! How was I to know who they would grow to be? It was protocol to give them to a royal family, and the Whites took them gleefully. They were my first case!"

"You knew who they would grow to be. You told me yourself you saw something evil within them. Yet you gave them to that family to cause destruction and ruin for generations! You insisted we give them a chance, insisted they could do great things and walk another path. You refused to see the truth. But you see everything, don't you, my dear sister? You see what a girl will become before she even knows it herself. You saw it in Maleficent, and you saw it in Lucinda, Ruby, and Martha."

"And I see it in Circe and Tulip as well! Hasn't

my love and care for them redeemed me in any way? Don't you see this is all connected? I have paid for my mistakes. And I am doing my best to make amends. That is why it's so important we change the way the fairies direct their magic, to avoid the disaster we're facing with the odd sisters."

"What has any of this to do with the odd sisters?"

"Everything!" a sonorous new voice boomed, reverberating throughout the courtyard and shaking the cherry blossom tree branches. All the fairies looked up and saw Oberon standing there, towering above them, majestic and awe-inspiring, but with kind, fatherly eyes. "Nanny is right," he said. "The fairies need to extend their reach! And as much as I agree with Nanny that this is all tangled up with the odd sisters' story, at the moment we need to focus on this impending threat. We need to protect the Fairylands! The odd sisters have raised Maleficent from the dead, and she is on her way to destroy the Fairylands. And we need to protect ourselves and the witches in the dead woods."

"The dead woods? Never! Let the witches of the dead defend themselves! Maleficent is on her way here to destroy us and we need our forces here!" squealed the Fairy Godmother, making Nanny gasp.

"Circe and Snow White are in the dead woods, Sister! How could you say that?"

"If Circe chooses the dead woods over the Fairylands, then perhaps she is not worthy of our protection. Perhaps she is fated to break your heart, as all your witches have before her. As for Snow White, someone must conjure her back to her own kingdom at once! We can't let a princess be harmed in any way!"

"I see the time you've spent with your sister in Morningstar has done nothing to change your fairy-minded ways!" said Oberon, looking down on the Fairy Godmother with disappointment and sadness. But she faced him head-on, putting her hands on her hips defiantly.

"You have always taken Nanny's side, Oberon! Always. Even now, when she admits to her mistakes, you still take her side! After all I've done for the Fairylands, this is how you treat me!"

"That is the difference between you and your sister. She admits to, and has learned from, her mistakes. She wants to make things better. You, however, do not, and it breaks my heart. I have been so long away from the Fairylands I felt it wasn't my right to come and sit in judgment, but I see my guidance is much needed. It is time for all of you to put aside your differences and fight together to defend all our lands!"

The Fairy Godmother was incensed. "I have half a mind to step down and let you and Nanny rule the Fairylands! I am sick to death of being criticized for upholding our traditions that *you* laid out for us so many years ago!"

Oberon gave the Fairy Godmother a sad look. "I think that may be the wisest suggestion you have ever made."

Chapter XV

The Odd
Sisters' List

It was twilight in the dead woods. The sky was purple, and the stars were glowing in the mist that always hung low and heavy in that part of the many kingdoms. Snow White was alone in the morning room, surrounded by the piles of books. She was reading Lucinda's journal by candlelight, hoping to learn more about the odd sisters, something Circe could perhaps use to defeat her mothers.

Circe, Hazel, and Primrose had gone to the library to find some of Manea's old spell books, hoping to discover a spell that could help them, while

Snow searched the books she had brought with her from the odd sisters' house. It was starting to get dark, and Snow glanced out the windows, hoping Circe and her new friends would return soon. She opened an old journal and was met with pages of cryptic notes that she soon realized belonged to the odd sisters themselves.

Maleficent

— Dragon fairy-witch. Nanny's pet. Keep an eye on her.

— Visit the girl for her birthday. Command the stars! Break Nanny's heart and take the girl for ourselves.

— We love her! But there will be no cake. The stars are at our command. Watch Nanny's heart break.

— She didn't mean it! She didn't mean it! We didn't see. Our dearest dragon fairy-witch killed our Circe. She doesn't know! Never tell her! This is our fault for pushing the stars. We didn't see! We love her now even more.

⟶ We will bring our darling girl to us!
Yes. We will care for her! This is our fault.

⟶ She commands nature, but only in
darkness. Teach her to obscure the sun!
She will rule all.

⟶ We will share our secrets. We will bring
Circe and Maleficent's daughter together.

⟶ She has nothing left. She is losing
herself. She gave too much away. We are three
and she is one. We made a mistake. Her
daughter has taken her heart. She is powerful.
Her power is growing as her heart fades into
nothing. We love her more for it.

⟶ Maleficent says we are losing ourselves.
She says we've changed. Says it's degenerative.
She lies!

Ursula

~~Our greatest friend. A grand and terrible witch with great power. We love her.~~ Traitorous witch! We hate her! <u>She Must Die!</u>

Nanny

Fairy in the guise of a witch

Tulip

She's not the fool we thought she was.

Oberon

All is well while he sleeps.

Rock Giant

Use them against the Tree Lords.

Popinjay

— Foolish boy!

Grimhilde in the Mirror

— Use her to torture Snow.

The Fairies

— We will destroy them!

Primrose and Hazel

— Foul human girls! They are not Gothel's true sisters!

Jacob

— The witches' creature, watch him!

Tiddlebottom

~ She is no fool!

Teacup Spells

~ The teacups must be touched by the lips of the victim, else the spell will not be as effective. Drink from the cup and learn their secrets. Break the cup and they will be broken beyond repair. Fill the cup with water and the eye of an egg, and you will see them. Fill the cup with what frightens them most to give them nightmares. Bury the cup in cemetery dirt to suffocate them. Fill the cup with their blood mingled with your own to control them. Throw the cup into fire and send them to Hades. Toss it into the sea to give their soul to the sea witch.

Objects of our Desires

 Power

Insanity

 Heartbreak

Break the sisters' bond

 Envy

 Madness

 Insecurity

Shadowman

 He has his own will.

Snow White

- Terrible girl. Daughter to our cousin King White

- She will take from us what we cherish most.

- Must kill her!

- Visit the queen! Take the brat to the woods.

- Drive Grimhilde mad, drive her to kill Snow.

- Protected by Grimhilde

- Plague her dreams. Destroy her bond with Grimhilde. Use Circe.

⚜ ⚜ ⚜ ⚜

Snow slammed the book closed and set it down next to her. She was starting to get nervous. Where was Circe? Fidgety, she opened the book again and flipped back to the page she wanted to show her cousin. She couldn't stop thinking about it. What did Lucinda mean by using Circe to destroy her bond with her mother? Was all this part of the odd sisters' plan, then? Were they all just puppets in some play the odd sisters had written, as her mother had once said?

The feeling of nervousness came over Snow White again, and she started to feel like the walls were closing in on her. It was the same feeling she'd had when she was alone in the odd sisters' house. She stood up and was about to leave the room when the candles started to flicker and fade. The room was cold and oppressive, making Snow White shiver.

I told you never to trust a witch, my daughter.

Snow White jumped, looking around the room, but couldn't find where her mother's voice was coming from. The candlelight danced to the sound, throwing shadows across the walls.

Over here, my bird. Over here.

Snow followed the sound of her mother's voice; it was frightening to hear it in this strange dead place. A place for witches. Then she found her. Her mother's face was reflected in an oval mirror.

The mirror was situated on the far wall among portraits of the dead queens who had once ruled the dead woods. It was eerie seeing her mother among them. When Snow got closer to the altar, she realized the mirror was cracked, distorting her mother's grim face.

Look what that witch has done to me!

"Who did this to you?" Snow White was horrified to see her mother so altered.

Circe! She's broken my cup. I'm barely holding on, my bird. Don't trust her, Snow! Circe is being used by her mothers to destroy you. It was always you they hated. Always you they wanted dead. They used me to get to you, and when that didn't work, they used their own daughter.

"I don't believe you!"

I am being forced from my mirror, Snow! I will never see you again! Please get out of here while you can! They're coming.

"Circe didn't know breaking your cup would hurt you! She was angry with her mothers when she did it! She didn't know that would happen!"

Oh, didn't she? She's been trying to keep you from me since you went to Morningstar! She tells herself she is protecting you from me when she should be protecting herself from her own mothers! Vile hags, meddling, plotting, and ruining lives! You'd do well to leave this place before they rain terror on all your heads! They hate you, my bird, hate you because they foresaw how Circe would come to love you.

"None of this makes sense, Mother. You say they wanted me dead because of my friendship with Circe, yet you're telling me they've thrust us together? It's all madness!"

The odd sisters are mad. They are trapped in promises they can't escape. Now go. Go before they get here. I can't keep them back much longer. They're coming, my bird. They're coming. . . .

Before Snow could answer, the mirror started to shatter; her mother's screams were filled with terror and pain, mingling with the sound of breaking glass.

The glass exploded all over the room, slicing the arm Snow White was using to shield her face. When she raised her head from the crook of her arm, she saw her mother's body on the floor. She was covered with a pattern of gashes that looked like cracks in a mirror. "Mother! No!" screamed Snow, panicked by her mother's ghastly wounds.

Circe, Primrose, and Hazel rushed into the room. Snow saw the looks of horror on their faces when they spotted Grimhilde.

"Circe! Please help my mother! Quickly!"

Circe appeared to be frozen with fear and revulsion. "Circe! Please!" But Circe wasn't looking at Snow or her mother. She was looking past them, at the empty frame that had held the broken mirror. Something was crawling out of the frame, contorting its body like a sickening insect, horrific and monstrous. They heard the cracking of bones and the groans of more creatures coming forth from the mirror. Snow White and the witches watched in horror as they unfolded their bodies, straightening themselves to their full natural statures.

It was the odd sisters, lurid, vile, and wicked as ever.

"Oh dear. It looks like we've stumbled upon a witch's nest. Whatever shall we do?" The odd sisters laughed as Lucinda waved her hand, sending Hazel, Primrose, and Circe careering out of the room, and slamming the door after them.

"Excuse us, dears. We want to be alone with Snow White and her mother."

CHAPTER XVI

THE WITCH'S DAUGHTER

The odd sisters stood there, laughing at Snow White. They looked like strange creatures out of a nightmare. They were as hideous and unnatural as she remembered them.

Snow couldn't help feeling like she was dreaming. These witches had plagued her sleep since she was a small child, and now she was standing before them while her mother lay dying on the floor. She'd dreaded the day she might have to face the odd sisters again, and she'd always wondered what she would do if she did. But she found her voice somewhere within her, in a place she hadn't known existed. A place of strength and fortitude.

"Shut up, you harpies! What have you done to my mother?" Snow screamed.

The odd sisters sneered at Snow White. "Oh, so brave, so strong! Thank Circe for that, dear! Without her you would still be under your mother's dominion and hiding behind Verona's skirts!" Lucinda said, laughing at Snow White.

"Oh, you're a witch's daughter, all right. Just look at the way you glare at us. I thought you would be more afraid. I thought you would cower and cry like you did when you were a little girl," said Martha before Lucinda took over.

"Are you sure you want us to save your mother, dear? Do you really want to go back to your lands with your mother always watching you from behind the mirror? Trapped forever in the company of the woman who tried to kill you?"

"You made her do it! I read the book of fairy tales! I read your journals! I know the truth!"

Lucinda inched her way closer, her eyes locked on Snow. "So brave. You surprise me," said Lucinda.

Then, looking down at Grimhilde's bloody and broken body, she cackled. "Can you hear me, Grimhilde? Can you feel how frightened your daughter is? You wouldn't know it by the look on her face. You should be proud. She has found her hate at last.

"When was the last time you saw your own reflection in the mirror and not your mother's, Snow? She doesn't want you to know how beautiful you are! She never has! She's the same spiteful, hurtful witch she always was! Do you know she begged us to kill you? Begged us! So desperate to be rid of you so her father would call her the fairest in the lands. She wished for your death!" said Lucinda, taking delight in hurting Snow White.

"Shut your mouth! You did that to her! My mother loves me! She loves me now, and she loved me then."

"So she does. Loves you so much she trapped Maleficent's bird Opal, using the poor creature against her will so we could lure Maleficent from beyond the veil! And then your mother marveled in awe as she watched us use debased and black magic

233

to bring Maleficent's dragon form back to life! Loves you so much she helped Pflanze aid us in our escape from the land of dreams so we could raise Maleficent from the dead. All in exchange for *you*! She's been plotting and scheming with us without a care about who lives or dies in the process! So don't you see, my dear? Your mother is, and has always been, a witch. She is just like us."

"Lies!"

"Your mother came to us in the dreamscape! She begged us to help her! She agreed to do whatever it took as long as she had you back at home with her again. So who is lying, Snow White? I think it may be you who are lying to yourself!"

Snow White looked down at her mother. Her breathing was shallow and blood was starting to pour from the long slashes that covered her face and body. "She's dying, please help me!"

"Look at this. Snow White asking us for help? Asking the vile harpies who turned your mother against you to save her. What would King Charming think of that?"

But Snow wasn't listening; she was bent over her mother, trying to hear what she was saying. It was a small whisper, barely audible, like a small hiss.

"Come closer, my darling. I love you," said Grimhilde as her wounds started to crack open. She was falling apart like a shattered mirror, blood pooling all over the floor around her, making Snow White scream. Her mother was dead. Shattered into a million pieces. Snow had lost her forever. And to her surprise, underneath the horror, pain, and grief, she felt relief.

The odd sisters laughed as they watched Snow White looking down on her mother in horror. "Oh! We see into your heart, Snow White! Not so pure after all! We see the apple doesn't fall far from the tree! Wishing death upon your mother, we see!" The odd sisters spoke in sickening harmony.

"It's not true!" screamed Snow. "It's not true!"

"Speaking of apples," said Ruby. "Did you find the gift your mother left on our doorstep?" Snow White looked up at Ruby, disgusted by the delight she was taking in these horrors. "What are you saying?"

The odd sisters laughed again. "Who else would bring you such a nice red apple but your mother?"

Snow White stood up, her hands and the hem of her dress covered in her mother's blood. "Lies!" The odd sisters' laughter filled the room, and something about it made Snow White feel as if these wretched women were telling the truth. She hated to admit it, but she knew in her heart her mother had left the apple. She had felt the same way that day in the odd sisters' house that she felt right before her mother appeared this evening. Panic. The need to flee. But that feeling was gone. Dead with her mother. And with that she found a great sense of power within herself. She wasn't afraid of the odd sisters.

"Don't be a fool, Snow White. Witch's daughter or not, you have no power over us. No antidote. True love's first kiss will not help you to defeat these witches!" Martha said, cackling, as Lucinda grabbed Snow White by the throat and squeezed tightly.

Circe finally managed to burst through the door.

Her face contorted in horror as she saw what her mothers were doing to Snow. Hazel and Primrose followed, readying themselves for battle.

"Snow! The locket! Drink it!" screamed Circe. She and Hazel flung curses at Lucinda, but they only made Lucinda laugh more—that is until she heard choking noises coming from Ruby and Martha. They were being strangled by an invisible force. Lucinda released Snow at once, and Ruby and Martha fell to the ground as well, gasping for air. A look of utter disgust crossed Lucinda's face.

"What witchery is this?" she whispered, looking at Circe. "Did you do this?"

CHAPTER XVII

RETURN OF
THE QUEENS

Circe could feel her mothers' anger. It sent a chill throughout her body, making her shiver. The odd sisters were screaming so loudly she thought they would bring the mansion down around them.

"How dare you share your blood—*our* blood—with Snow White!" screamed Lucinda, her eyes blazing with anger. "You can't protect Snow White from us forever!" Then she turned to Snow White. "And you can't have her! Circe is ours! As she was meant to be! As she was designed to be! Together we will bring darkness into this world and we will sing and dance to the sounds of screams from the land of the living!"

"Daughter, stop this at once!" It was Jacob. He stood there, serene and composed. Stoic and fatherly. Lucinda stopped cold. Her face crumbled into that of a little girl being scolded.

"Father?" Lucinda whispered, her voice so small that it seemed unnatural.

Circe had never seen her mother so passive. A calmness came over Lucinda, as if seeing her father somehow brought her out of her madness, if only for a moment. Martha and Ruby looked transfixed, their heads tilted to one side, their eyes too wide, and their mouths agape. Something about the man calmed her mothers, bringing them back to the edge of sanity and making Circe remember why she loved them.

"Calm yourself, my precious girl. All this rage and anger. You're too much like your mother and grandmother. You must learn to quiet your souls," Jacob cooed, trying to soothe his daughters.

"Don't speak to me of my mother and grand-mother! They cast us away, sending us off to live with the fairies and into the hands of the One of Legends! You realize that is how she got her name, don't you? It wasn't coined because of her greatness!" said Lucinda, her madness returning.

"We didn't want to send you away! We had no choice, my girl! I promise you it was the last thing your mother and I wanted to do!"

Circe could see her mothers slipping into and out of sanity. She saw the madness washing over their faces, overtaking them like a foul demon, and releasing them again when they heard Jacob's voice. It was the strangest thing she had ever beheld, her mothers' transforming like this before her eyes, returning to their former selves. She wanted Snow out of the room, away from her mothers. *Hazel, take Snow down to my mothers' house.* Hazel nodded, hearing Circe's thoughts. While the odd sisters were still being lulled by Jacob, she took Snow by the hand and led her out of the room.

"Mothers, listen to Jacob, please!" cried Circe. "He loves you. I know he does. Just listen to him," she said as Jacob slowly made his way to his broken daughters, approaching them tentatively, like they were wild beasts that could attack at any moment.

"Lucinda, my girl. Can I please hold your hand? I felt so ashamed after I shunned you and your sisters all those years ago, when you came to the dead woods. But I was afraid."

"I didn't know who you were that day," said Lucinda. Her eyes welled with tears. "We didn't learn who you were until we read Manea's journals many years later."

"My daughters, please sit down with me. There's so much I have to tell you. Come, let us sit and talk somewhere we will be comfortable."

Lucinda, Ruby, and Martha let Jacob lead them into the large dining room. Circe watched, stunned at how calm they were in his presence. How willing they were to do as he asked.

"Come along, my little girls," he said as he helped them to their seats, pulling a chair out for each of them, treating them as cherished daughters with tender touches and a loving look in his eyes. Circe stood in the doorway with Primrose, amazed by the scene, waiting for something to go wrong, worried the odd sisters would fall back into delirium, worried Hazel wouldn't get Snow White to the safety of the odd sisters' house before the odd sisters lost their minds again. "My girls, sit down. I need you to listen to me. All of you," he said, looking at them.

Circe and Primrose took seats across from the odd sisters, eyeing the doorway as they waited for Hazel to return. Jacob was sitting at the head of the table, and the stone harpies that dominated the room loomed over them. He was smiling at Lucinda, lost in the beauty of her face, lost in the memories of their mother. "You're so much like them, my daughter, so much like your mother and her mother," he said, looking at all the witches. "And when I was brought back to life as a servant to the queens of the dead woods, and you were made three, I loved you even more. But the ancestors were angry with your grandmother for her plots to extend her reach outside of the dead woods and became convinced you would do the same. They foresaw that you would

243

destroy the dead woods if allowed to stay within its thicket. I see now how mistaken they were." Jacob seemed to drift off into a place only he could see, a place they couldn't follow him to. Perhaps he was remembering those days, or perhaps he was just happy to be in the company of his brood of witches.

"Your grandmother Nestis once tried to extend her reach beyond the dead woods, just as you are trying to do. She wanted to make the world black, to unleash her creatures on the many kingdoms, but the ancestors stopped her and forced your mother to give you to the fairies. They convinced her it was the only choice."

"But why didn't you fight to keep us here? Why didn't Mother?" Lucinda asked. She seemed like a lost, lonely child, not the terrible witch she had become.

"We did, my girl, we did! But your mother wasn't strong enough. Not yet. She hadn't come into her full powers, and by the time she was strong, she believed the ancestors. She found herself fearing you as much as the ancestors had. But I see now we should have kept you here, kept you close. We should never have unleashed you on the many kingdoms only to cause havoc and destruction! If it were up to your mother and I, you would have ruled here after your mother passed, not Gothel, not that poor wretched child, or her sisters here, as much as I love them."

"Then why didn't you tell us all of this when we visited here?" asked Ruby, not looking as convinced as her sister Lucinda that her father was telling the truth.

"Because, my girl, I believed the ancestors. And your mother believed them. I thought you would be the ruin of this place. I was bound to protect Gothel, as I am bound to protect all queens and future queens of the dead, and to keep my mistresses' secrets." Jacob gathered the odd sisters' hands and took them into his own. "Oh, my poor girls, you have been wandering the many kingdoms lost, forever searching for your true home, acting out your nature, the nature you inherited from your mother and her mother before her."

Circe sat quietly, listening to Jacob. He was right. It made sense that her mothers would want to create a daughter in the same fashion their own mother had. But they had gone about it the wrong way. They had given too much of themselves away. They had lost too much.

"If you had been raised here, you would live within the confines of the dead woods. Here you would have had a purpose, a place to rule. The ancestors never should have tossed you into the unsuspecting world, where you are just chaos and destruction. Here you would have ruled after your mother."

"You say our grandmother made us into three. What do you mean?" Martha asked, staring at Jacob with wide eyes. She seemed to be examining his every detail, as if the answer could be found in his face.

"What does he mean, Lucinda?" Ruby chimed in. They became manic, and Lucinda saw them spiraling into the same insanity that seemed to seize them more frequently than ever. "What does he mean?" they screamed, standing up and ripping

246

at their black dresses and pulling at the feathers in their hair, tossing them onto the floor, and scratching at their own faces.

"Sisters, stop this at once! You will ruin the dresses I only just conjured for us before we left the place between. You don't want to do that, do you? You don't want to ruin your pretty new dresses." Lucinda tried to calm her sisters in the best way she knew how.

Ruby and Martha stopped their fussing, but they still wanted to know what Jacob meant. "Lucinda, please tell us what he means. We don't understand."

"My dear sisters. My Ruby and Martha. I was born of our mother, Manea, and Jacob's love, and Nestis, our grandmother, split me into three, creating you. She created you the same way we created Circe and helped Maleficent to create Aurora, don't you see?"

"But it wasn't quite the same spell, though, was it, Lucinda?" It was Hazel. She had been listening at the doorway, about to come in. Lucinda snapped her head around to look at Hazel.

"Another human with a witch's blood! Blasphemous!" spat Lucinda. "At least Gothel was created by magic! We were her true sisters! Sisters in magic! You and your sister Primrose were taken from the village as babies by Jacob, did you know that? Taken away from your real parents, nasty human parents, and given Manea's blood! To replace us! I should kill you where you stand!"

"You know that is impossible, Lucinda. We share the same blood. The blood of our mother!" Primrose stood up, clenching her fists around hexes, ready to defend her sister.

"Stop this, girls! Stop it at once!" Jacob's voice boomed, but the witches wouldn't hear him. Everything had fallen into delirium again. All the witches were wailing and screaming at each other.

"Did you know who you were when you came to us so many years ago? Is that why you took our sister Gothel from us and helped in destroying the dead woods?" asked Hazel, not hiding her contempt for Lucinda and her sisters.

"We took her because she was our true sister.

Not like you. She was created with magic in the old way, as it was done for generations by the queens of the dead woods! We wanted her for ourselves. We wanted our family back!" hissed Lucinda, clenching her fists, digging them into her own flesh with anger.

"And then you abandoned her! You left her to go mad and wither to a husk while trying to bring us back, stringing her along for years, making her believe you would help her!"

"We wanted to help her! We tried. But we had to find a way to bring Circe back! We had to save Maleficent."

"But if you had just used our mother's spells, the spells used for generations by our ancestors, and not tampered with them, none of this would have happened. Instead you took our mother's spell and made it your own! You twisted it and turned it into something destructive, like everything you touch, Lucinda. We loved you when you came to the dead woods, you know we did! You could have told us who you were and stayed to live here with us. We could have been happy together. We loved you so well, Lucinda. We were happy to have other witches in the dead woods. Someone to teach us magic. But you used Gothel, took our spells and twisted them, making them rebound on you and your dragon fairy-witch, and destroyed everything in the process!"

"It wasn't our fault! It was a miscalculation! We are three, Maleficent was just one, that's why it rebounded on her!"

"But don't you see the same thing has been happening to you, just much more slowly? You gave Circe everything that was good within you, and because you are three, the degenerative effects simply took longer to destroy you! Don't you see, Lucinda, you're all going insane. My sister Gothel saw it. So did Maleficent and Ursula, they all said so in their missives. They saw it happening slowly over the years. And surely Circe sees it now. The only ones who don't see it are you."

"Don't speak to us of Ursula! She is a traitorous witch and deserved her foul death!"

"That may be so, but she loved you well before

she lost her mind, did she not? Don't you see you have been sailing perilously close to the same depths of madness for many years? Please, Lucinda. Don't do this. Don't destroy everyone your daughter loves just to keep her close. With every person you hurt and life you destroy, you punish your daughter. You punish Circe."

The odd sisters crumbled into madness once again. "No! Not punishment! She's our light. Like Aurora was Maleficent's. To have her near is to have our light back. The farther away she is, the less we can see clearly. We need our light. Otherwise we are in darkness and we are alone."

"Mothers, I am here. No one is going to take me away from you," said Circe, feeling she needed to say something to calm her mothers. But she couldn't face a life by their side, not as they were now. And she was more certain than ever about what she had to do.

"These witches would have you to themselves! And so would Nanny, and the fairies! Everyone wants to take you from us! Nanny thinks she can make up for her past deeds by protecting you! Protecting you from us! But we won't have it! We made a promise, a promise in hate that we are bound to fulfill! We are trapped in the promise we made in the land of dreams. We will have you for ourselves, Circe! We will rip from you everyone you hold dear so that you have only us!" Lucinda was raving, her hair wild and her face distorted by her mania.

The odd sisters stood together, raising their arms. Small balls of silver light appeared in their hands, crackling and emitting sparks throughout the room as they grew. The odd sisters squeezed the shining spheres, causing lightning to burst from their fists. It struck the walls and sent tremors throughout the entire mansion. The lightning struck the oldest parts of the mansion, bringing life to the stone carvings of night creatures that slumbered within. The creatures broke free, causing the mansion to crumble. The harpies that dominated the dining room came to life and crashed through the large picture windows, shattering the glass and falling to the courtyard below. Circe, Primrose, and

Hazel screamed as Lucinda commanded the creatures of the dead woods.

"Night creatures, do my bidding! This is your queen! Seek out my enemies in the Fairylands and the many kingdoms, and destroy them all in my name!"

The mansion started to rumble and shake again; everyone in the room could hear the sounds of stone cracking and crashing to the ground. Jacob, Primrose, Hazel, and Circe all ran to the windows and saw giant stone dragons circling the dead woods. They saw the Gorgon statue come to life and walk through the courtyard toward a giant crimson spiral of light right at the boundary of the dead woods. Stone ravens and crows were circling above the Gorgon as more stone harpies crashed through windows, joining the other winged creatures that were making their way out of the dead woods.

Circe closed her eyes and sighed. She knew what she had to do. She'd known it since she started her journey, and only now would she have the courage to do it.

CHAPTER XVIII

WAR IN THE FAIRYLANDS

Oberon and his Tree Lords were assembled on the boundaries of the Fairylands. They were ready and waiting to fight Maleficent should she return. Oberon's heart was filled with dread at the thought of facing her again, and at the same time filled with joy at seeing his fairies gathered together in the distance, on the lookout for Maleficent.

He had lost many friends and soldiers in their last battle with Maleficent. His lost friends would return, of course, but not for many years, not until they'd had time enough to grow. Tulip had seen to the replanting of his fallen Tree Lords after the battle at Morningstar. She had put their roots back into the ground and tended to them with care. But now she had an even more important task given to her, one that filled Oberon's heart with worry.

He felt he should have seen this coming—a great war between the witches and fairies. But he hoped they would be spared. As he and his army stood guard, waiting for the battle to commence, he put out a silent call to all the gods of nature to help in the battle. He knew the odd sisters would not stop after destroying the Fairylands; they would want dominion over the entirety of the many kingdoms now that they had taken their place as queens of the dead. He had tried to reason with Manea and her mother years ago, tried to convince them that sending Lucinda and her sisters into the world would be a mistake, but they hadn't listened. It had been his experience that most did not listen when oracles of another faith spoke their truth. They listened only to their own kind. He often felt he should have refused to take the odd sisters in, giving the witches of the dead woods no choice other than to raise the children themselves, but he had feared for the children's fates and decided to take the tiny witches in and arrange a proper home for them.

Nanny had seemed like the right fairy to undertake such an untraditional role, but all fell into chaos, grief, and ruin as she suffered one loss after another, until she finally decided to lose herself in the place between. That was when Oberon took away Nanny's memories. Took her identity, giving her peace and a chance to redeem herself through Tulip and Circe.

And now here they were, both faced with the possibility of having to destroy these witches because of the choices they had made along with their parents. As he looked at Nanny, standing with her sister and the other fairies ready for battle, he felt a deep sorrow for her that she might have to face her foster daughter in strife once again. He felt himself pulled in many directions, his mind drifting from his soldiers to his fairies and to Circe. He wanted to send part of his army to the dead woods, but there were so few soldiers left now after their last battle with Maleficent that he felt they were needed here. He could only hope the gods of nature would listen to his call and come to Circe's aid in the dead woods—if it wasn't too late already.

Oberon watched the sky for Maleficent's bird, Opal. She was keeping a lookout for any sign of Maleficent and the odd sisters' other creatures. The Fairy Godmother, Flora, Merryweather, Fauna, Nanny, and the Blue Fairy, with a legion of other fairies, were in the distance, just beyond the horizon, keeping watch as well. He was so proud seeing all his fairies assembled on the hilltop, standing together side by side, their wands ready to do battle with Maleficent once again. He could see Nanny searching the sky for Opal with her keen eyes, hoping she would bring an early warning of Maleficent's arrival. As brave as his fairies were, he knew they dreaded another confrontation with the Dark Fairy. Especially Nanny.

He thanked the Fairylands for Opal. Before she came to him with the odd sisters' plans, he had thought the poor creature had died along with Maleficent's other birds during the great battle. It was a brave choice, coming to him as she had, making Grimhilde and Lucinda's plan known to him after she escaped Grimhilde's clutches. He knew what it meant for Opal to betray her old mistress, but Opal had watched Maleficent change over her many years; she no longer saw the young girl she used to love within Maleficent before she died. And now that her tormented mistress was finally released from her pain, Opal had turned her loyalties to a witch with a pure heart. Circe.

Oberon sighed, remembering how desperate Opal was when she told him her tale. She had survived the battle, but hid among Maleficent's dead ravens and crows to see if she could find her mistress. But what she found was the odd sisters plotting to raise her mistress from the dead, to use her as they had longed to do while she was alive, and she knew she had to stop them. The poor bird had gone through so much while making her way to him, and he hoped she would survive this battle to share her story with Circe herself. He hoped they would all survive. Either way their story would live on in the book of fairy tales, as all their stories had, if readers looked deep enough. Surely the book would contain the story of how the old queen Grimhilde had captured poor Opal. Or how Snow White was finally free of her mother. Or how the odd sisters had used old and sinister magic to bring Maleficent back from the dead. Or the story of a brave young woman named Tulip who made peace between the Cyclopean Giants and the Tree Lords. All their stories were there, written or waiting to be written. And he wondered what ending Circe would write for herself.

And then he saw. His answer was there, silhouetted and falling from the clouds, careering toward the earth. The dark shadowy dragon beast was plummeting to its death. The odd sisters had brought her back only for her to die another painful death, and he knew without a doubt what a grave mistake he had made in letting the odd sisters live outside the dead woods' boundaries. And he knew what Circe must have done to save them all.

CHAPTER XIX

THE WITCH'S SACRIFICE

Circe had taken the small mirror from her pocket and broken it. No one noticed in the confusion and mayhem. Her mothers were ranting, and Jacob was trying in vain to calm his daughters, but their madness had overcome them, and they could no longer hear their father's words. Hazel and Primrose had run down to the odd sisters' house in the courtyard to see if Snow White had been injured by the falling stones when the harpies came to life, leaving Jacob and Circe alone with the odd sisters.

Circe looked down at the broken mirror. She could see Snow's face reflected in the broken pieces.

She is safe. Primrose and Hazel will take care of her, she thought. *At least Snow will be safe.*

Then she wiped the broken pieces of mirror so she didn't have to see her cousin's face in the long sharp piece she grasped in her hand.

She was so afraid. But she didn't have a choice. It was the only way to make her mothers whole again. It was the only way to bring back their sanity.

She took the long, jagged piece of glass and plunged it into her heart. She felt herself choking on blood as she began to lose her vision. The last thing she saw before she closed her eyes was her mothers' horrified faces. She heard them screaming as her world went black.

⚜ ⚜ ⚜ ⚜

Snow White, Primrose, and Hazel returned to a nightmare. Primrose and Hazel stood, stunned, while Snow gathered Circe in her arms. She looked as if she was drowning in sorrow. Too grief-stricken to cry, she sat there wondering how this could have happened.

Primrose reached out and touched Snow on the shoulder tenderly, trying to comfort her. Jacob closed his eyes, willing away his tears, not wanting to see Circe's lifeless face. He tended to his daughters, who were lying on the floor, motionless but still breathing.

"This isn't how it was supposed to end!" said Snow, looking up at Primrose, her cheek covered in Circe's blood. As Primrose's heart broke for the woman, she thought this was probably the only way it could have ended, but she had hoped with all her heart it wouldn't have to.

Hazel joined Jacob and sat down next to the odd sisters. "There is nothing of the madness left within them. Circe has saved them from their madness by giving them back the best parts of themselves, I can feel it. I wonder why they won't wake."

"I don't think they wish to live in a world without their daughter." Jacob stood up to look out the windows at the broken landscape. The ground was covered in rubble from the night creatures that had fallen to the ground the moment Circe took her own life. "She's saved us all, you realize. The Fairylands, everyone in the many kingdoms, all with her sacrifice."

Snow White stood up quite suddenly. Her face was ghastly pale, but she was almost elated. "The flowers! We can take her to the flowers!" Jacob and the witches said nothing. They just looked at Snow sadly. "Come on! We have to take her to Gothel's old house! The flowers are there. We can bring her back to life!" Snow didn't understand why no one was saying anything. Why no one saw this was the solution.

Primrose leaned down and put her arm around Snow. "We can't, my darling. If we do, then Lucinda and her sisters will return to bedlam." Snow White stood up, noticing the blood on her dress for the first time. She didn't know which was Circe's and which was her own, or what she found more revolting: being covered in the blood of her dearest friend or the idea that the odd sisters would live and Circe would not. She couldn't let this be the end. She couldn't lose Circe. Not now. She suddenly understood how the odd sisters had felt when they lost Circe years before. The sense of desperation to get her back was overwhelming. They had just found each other. They had just become friends.

"Then we kill the odd sisters!" Snow said, surprising herself.

"You *are* a witch's daughter," said Hazel. "But Circe has made her choice. She could have killed her mothers—she had the power to do so even if she didn't know it herself—but she chose to sacrifice herself so they could live. She knew that taking her own life would restore their greatest virtues."

"But it's not fair! I can't lose her, I can't!"

Hazel smiled at Snow and said, "Everything you loved about Circe is now within her mothers. She was special because her mothers made her that way."

Snow White was angrier than she'd ever been. "It shouldn't have to be like this! I refuse to accept it! There has to be another way!"

Primrose took Snow by the hand. "You have to, my dear. Circe wanted this. She felt it was her fault that her mothers fell into delirium. This was Circe's choice to make, and it was foreseen by the ancestors. We have to honor that."

Snow White shook her head. "Curse the ancestors! I can't believe you're okay with this! I thought you wanted to help Circe! I thought she had finally found a home and a family in you and in this place! I know that is how you felt as well! I could see it when you looked at her! Tell me you are okay with her choice, tell me you didn't wish for things to be different, and I will drop this."

Hazel sighed and joined them, putting her arm around Snow. "Of course we hoped things would go differently. We love Circe. We loved her long before we laid eyes on her, from the moment we first heard her voice in the place between. And yes, we wanted her to live here with us, to live out her life with us in the dead woods, and that was a path she could have taken. A path the ancestors hoped she would take. But that meant killing her mothers. And only Circe could make that choice. We couldn't force that upon her."

Snow White couldn't help feeling there was another way. "I know in my heart this isn't how it's supposed to end. I know it! Why can't any of you see that?"

The room became infused with light as a new

voice echoed in the room. Calm and serene, it was the voice of the ancestors.

Snow White is right. This is not how it has to end.

"Gothel?" Primrose looked around the room, trying to find the source of the voice.

Gothel is with us, Primrose, and we speak as one, as the ancestors of the dead woods have always done.

The light in the room intensified.

Circe should not have to die for our mistakes. And neither should her mothers. The choice will be theirs to make together.

Snow felt strange talking to an invisible being, to this otherworldly voice, but she found her courage and asked, "But how? How will they make the choice?"

We will speak to them, Snow White. They will be given a choice. A choice only they can make. They will decide what to do, and we will honor it and use our powers to enforce their will. We promise you.

"I don't understand! How will they know they have the choice? How will we know what they want?"

They are in the place between, and they are listening.

CHAPTER XX

HOME

Circe and the odd sisters were sitting at their table in the kitchen in front of the large round window. Outside, they had a view of Maleficent's crows perched peacefully in the apple tree.

Siting on the table was a magnificent birthday cake, and Mrs. Tiddlebottom was puttering around in the kitchen, making tea.

"Where are we?" Circe asked, confused.

Mrs. Tiddlebottom laughed. "I don't know, dear. I thought you would tell me."

"We're in the place between," said Lucinda.

Circe hadn't thought it would look like this, the place between.

"It looks any way we wish, Daughter," said Ruby, putting a saucer of milk on the floor for Pflanze.

"Pflanze!" Circe was happy to see her until she realized what it meant. "Oh, Pflanze. Are you okay?" The cat didn't answer.

"She can't speak with you, darling. She is too weak. She is barely holding on, but we will do what we can to keep her here, won't we? We won't let her pass beyond the veil, not for us. Just as we won't let you go into the mists with our ancestors."

Circe suddenly felt as if she were young again, sitting with women she thought were her sisters in the kitchen on a bright sunny morning. She was so happy she had made the right choice. She was happy to see her mothers this way, as they were meant to be.

"We, too, are happy to be ourselves again," said Lucinda. "But we wish it didn't take your death to achieve it."

Mrs. Tiddlebottom brought the witches a pot of

tea and some cups. "Here you go, dears," she said, putting down the tray. Circe looked up at her.

"Oh! Mrs. T! What are you going to do? Move forward beyond the veil or back to your old life?"

Mrs. Tiddlebottom laughed. "I've lived far too long already, but the ancestors have one more task for old Mrs. Tiddlebottom before she goes. I'm to look after the flowers should you and your mothers decide to use them. I've only just stopped by from my own corner of the place between for a spot of tea before I make my way back home. And to ask you a favor."

Circe smiled. "Of course, what's the favor?" But Lucinda answered for the old woman.

"She would like us to make our choice quickly. She is ready to go beyond the veil." Lucinda smiled at Mrs. Tiddlebottom. "I'm sorry our ancestors have interfered with your passing."

Mrs. Tiddlebottom patted Lucinda on the shoulder. "Oh, you're not the same witch I remember. Not at all. I like this version of you much better."

Lucinda laughed. "I like myself better, too."

"But what choice are we talking about? I've already made my choice! And why are you here, Mothers? Why aren't you in the dead woods? Why aren't you living the lives I gave you with the sacrifice of my own?"

Lucinda took Circe's hand.

"Because, my Circe, we are in the place between, and we have been given a choice. And all we have to do is listen to hear it."

THE END